BETRAYED

ROSS GALLEN

Kravitz & Sons

INNOVATORS IN PUBLISHING, MARKETING AND ADVERTISING

Kravitz and Sons LLC
204 E Arlington Blvd. Suite B
Greenville, NC 27858

This is a work of fiction. The story is imaginary and any resemblance to real people, events, or places is coincidental.

Published by Kravitz and Sons LLC.

"Spy Thriller and Political Terrorism Fiction"

ISBN: 979-8-89639-553-9 (sc)
ISBN: 979-8-89639-554-6 (e)

Because of the dynamic nature of the Internet, any web addresses or links contained in this book may have changed since publication and may no longer be valid. The views expressed in this work are solely those of the author and do not necessarily reflect the views of the publisher, and the publisher hereby disclaims any responsibility for them.

TABLE OF CONTENTS

Life is a journey,

Life is a rhyme,

Life is what we laugh at all of the time.

CHAPTER 1

LIFE ON THE SEVENTEENTH floor of the National Bank Building at Fashion Island was good. My office fronted on the view of the harbour, with its vast expanse of small craft idling in the gentle motion of the waves. While the nameplate on the outside wall by my door simply said 'Jake Mandel', anyone who understood the protocols of a successful law firm would have instantly known by my corner office that I was a senior partner.

Even though my office was isolated at the far end of our firm's floor, I could hear the underlying electrical buzz of the printers as they pumped out the paper documents that were the lifeblood of our firm.

The door to my office was slightly ajar and I could see the secretaries and paralegals as they scurried about to create more paper. Paper was good because it meant our firm was prospering and our lifestyle would be maintained. Our large corporate clients were the cannon meat that powered the engine. We were merely a petty expense that allowed them to perpetrate their corporate greed.

Conversely, those of us at the top of the food chain enjoyed a luxurious lifestyle and provided employment for the underlings. I guess it was a matter of whose ox was being gored.

I felt pretty good as the sun streamed in and warmed my office. I could sense the rhythm of the workplace and took comfort in knowing that entrepreneurial capitalism, as we practiced it, was alive and well.

Adjusting the volume on my stereo system, I listened to the haunting sounds of Rachmaninoff's First Symphony. It had a certain melancholic resonance that was reminiscent of bringing yourself close to a climax, suddenly stopping for a breath of air, only to resume again.

I wasn't really working hard anymore. I put in long hours, but I was now skilled at my trade, and on top of the learning curve. Work was more a matter of network management than anything else. I was looking forward to my tryst with Silvie in the afternoon. Married life had long ceased to be anything other than a matter of appearance. Our marital bed was cold. I actually enjoyed sleeping alone in the guestroom. I did not have to listen to my wife's snoring and occasional farting in the middle of the night.

Our relationship was polite and formal. It allowed me access to the old GOP guard in a community that harped on about family values. The relationship was a necessity because business was done at social events, and appearance rather than actual propriety, was the order of the day.

Romantic love and marital fidelity were merely matters of lip service and appearance. All that really mattered was personal satisfaction and the feel of soft skin possessed by the young.

Leslie broke my comfortable mood as she plunged into my office, newspaper in hand. I shifted my gaze to her and found myself staring at her presence. It took me a moment to bring her into focus.

Leslie was my eyes and ears in the office. I had long since ceased to trust the integrity of my partners, and recognized they would sell me out for a farthing, or less. Somewhere along the line they had become so greedy that the only end game was how much money could be accumulated. I needed Leslie to keep me apprised of the interactions and schemes that took place at the water cooler. She was a loyal retainer, but came with a price. Yet, I was more than willing to pay it.

I tried to sort out what she was saying but my head was still full from last night's Jack Daniels. Holding up the morning paper she asked, "Have you seen the headline? Charlie Stewart's son was arrested for murder."

I could feel the wheels begin to turn in my head as I blankly stared at Leslie.

"What the fuck? Give me the paper!"

She quickly walked to my side and obliged. Taking the front page in my hands, I read that the son of the local GOP Chairman elect had been arrested for the murder of a four month old infant whose mother was his girlfriend. All it mentioned was that the baby had been taken to Huntington-West Hospital with serious head injuries, allegedly caused by Trey Stewart. The Huntington Beach Police were cooperating with the Orange County Sheriff in the investigation of the crime.

I could smell trouble coming. Charlie Stewart was a facilitator. He wasn't a business man, more like a con-man who appeared to have access to all of the economic notables in the community. He bridged the gap between the rich and the rich, and brought them together under a shared ideology of profit and greater profits.

The case was serious because Charlie was a one man band. Damage to his family could impact our practice. I immediately called a partnership meeting.

Orange County had always been a boar's nest of political alliances. In the days of the 'good old boys' the County was run by the John Birchers. They looked for communists under every rock and were suspicious of any rationally based political views. Their policy was to denounce and exclude anyone who did not adhere to the Bircher view. In a sense they were the ultimate extension of McCarthyism, cloaked in a garb of patriotism and love of country. The reality was they were just a bunch of bigots who wore suits instead of white hoods, and drove Mercedes instead of riding horses. The net impact was pretty much the same.

Their methodology was to divide, conquer, then exclude from the political process anyone who did not go along with their agenda. Their view of the world was consistent with Nixon's list of enemies.

Every family had its own skeletons, but a code of silence and failure of inquiry resulted in lack of exposure and papered over indiscretion and abuses.

With the influx of Asians, Hispanics and people of more liberal persuasion, cracks appeared in the old political structure. Those who were financially well endowed divided the political pie by seizing the party structure of the Democratic and Republican Parties.

As a practical matter, there was not a nickels worth of difference between the parties. Ideological differences were exposed to the public but, in the financial corridors of the county, the same families met and bred with each other as if there was no difference other than who was going to eat the political pie.

CHAPTER 2

MOHSEN OVASI WAS A decent man. His name portended what he ultimately became. In Farsi, Mohsen meant 'one who does good'.

A sickly childhood caused him to turn inward to the world of books. As much as he wanted to play on the soccer field with other boys of his age, a restrictive airway disease took its toll of his physical abilities.

By the time he matriculated from high school, he had assumed a bookish appearance and had developed an enormous appetite for science and western literature. Coming from a poor family he had little real expectation of receiving an academic education.

However, life in Iran was changing. The Shah made it possible for academically talented poor children to receive an academic education; if the education would further the interest of his regime.

Early on, Mohsen developed an acute understanding of Persian History. He understood that Iran, as a nation state, was one of the world's oldest continuous civilizations. He appreciated the fact that the Islamization of Iran did not take place until the 10th century, and was accompanied by the decline of the Zoroastrian religion. He silently believed that Islamization was a thin veneer and that it, too, would pass in time.

Life under the Shah was bringing Iran into the 20th Century. There were, of course, problems. Even though Iran was becoming proficient in western technology, the Shah's regime was the equivalent of living in a police state whose rules were enforced by the CIA and

MI5. The French influence had long since faded by the time of the late 1960's.

Mohsen finished his medical studies at what used to be known as Dar al-Funum—before the name of the medical school was changed to the University of Tehran.

All around him Mohsen saw unrest and firebrand religious leaders who sought to take the country back to the time of the Caliphate. He, and others, looked to the President of the United States for moral authority and military support; but only perceived a timid man who was long on rhetoric and fearful of the exercise of power. He often wondered to himself, what had happened to the Roosevelts and Trumans of this world? How could the Americans have elected a President who was such a spineless political hack?

Unrest was growing on the streets and Mohsen was fearful. He went to see his elderly parents.

His father told him, "Mohsen, you must go. I am just a simple man, but I know in my heart Tehran will never be a safe place for you. I can feel the anger in the people. Something bad is going to happen. You have to get out while it is still possible."

Mohsen looked at his parents. They were two frail, old people. A strong wind would have blown them away. Their time was short. They had no one except him. He could feel the tears as they started to streak down his face.

"But Baba who will be here for you, if not me? What will become of you?"

His father took his arm and looked deeply into his eyes.

"Mohsen, we've lived our lives. We are old. We are the past. You are the future. You are our only link to the future. We will survive through you. You must go!"

With that his father turned and took Mamma from the room. The discussion was over.

Standing in line at The British Embassy, Mohsen smiled at the Iranian clerk working at the visa desk. She was dark skinned with pitch black hair. She wasn't as dark as Mohsen, but it was clear that, even though she spoke with a marvellous British accent, she was not an Anglo-Saxon.

"You'll do well in England."

"They have a shortage of doctors and I'm sure you'll find a place. I wish I was getting out of here but, at least I have a stable job in a nice embassy, away from all the turmoil that's going around."

"Yes, thank you," he replied. "How long do you think it will be before I get my visa?"

"I'm sure it will be quick."

Mere days later, as he sat on the tarmac waiting for the 727 to take off, Mohsen felt subdued; naked against the world. Revolution was in the wind and his was on one of the last flights out of Tehran. Soon the dreaded religious police of the Islamic Republic would take over. He never saw his parents again; only left with a handful of faded black and white photographs.

Mohsen applied to the University of London for a post graduate position. Looking around the city, he felt he did not fit in. He stood out in stark contrast to the anglophiles. His impression was that they sneered down at him because of his swarthy appearance. As much as he tried, he could not integrate himself into the community. He felt he would always be an outsider from Iran, while his colleagues were the loyal subjects of the Queen.

He began to believe that only in America was there a place for him. America was after all, a multi-racial society and there was room for everyone.

Finally, obtaining a visa to The United States, he found himself not knowing much about the country. Yet, he applied to the University of Mississippi Medical School for an academic position and, receiving a warm letter from the Dean, decided to make the journey to Jackson, Mississippi.

Approaching the Dean's Office, he introduced himself to the Dean's secretary.

"Good morning. I am Mohsen Ovasi, here to see the Dean."

She looked up at him in quizzical fashion, "Just a moment please. I'll let him know you're here."

She returned a few minutes later, "I'll show you into his office now."

With that, she led him through the corridor into a magnificently panelled room with plaques and paraphernalia representing a lifetime's achievement.

"Dr. Ovasi," the Dean exclaimed, "so good of you to come. I've read your papers and am familiar with your work. Great work!"

Mohsen felt a sense of relief when he heard the kind words of the Dean. Perhaps he had at last found a place to alight.

After a few minutes of polite exchanges, the Dean's face took on a serious look.

"Dr. Ovasi, I regret to say it, but I don't think we have a place for you. You see, it's just a few years since we've had desegregation. You know, the James Meredith mess. This is the old south and, frankly, doctor, it's nothing against you, but you're so dark. The public is going to accuse us of hiring a Negro on the medical faculty and we're just not ready to deal with that issue. You do understand, don't you? I know you're not a Negro, but how do I explain that to the rest of the Mississippians? It just won't fly. I am so sorry, but I do have to be practical and keep in mind the best interests of the school."

Mohsen sat frozen in stunned silence. He could not believe what he was hearing. He thought to himself, this is America; the Dean is an educated man. Surely this could not be the case. *Is there no place in this world without bigots?* Wearily, he picked himself up and left the campus.

Looking back, Mohsen could not remember how he got on the plane to New York. He was seated next to a middle aged couple and guessed the woman to be about fifty whilst her husband looked a few years older. The woman wore a Hamsa around her neck. He recognized the symbol and thought perhaps it was a sign from home.

Starting a conversation, he said, "I see you wear a Hamsa for good luck."

In a distinctive upstate New York accented voice, she replied, "Oh, yes. I got it when we were in Tel Aviv. It's never been off my neck since."

He thought, *They must be Jewish.* He had never known Jewish people and wondered if it was true that they hated all Iranians.

It turned out the woman's husband was a neonatologist at Strong Memorial Hospital in Rochester, New York. When Mohsen told them his story, they looked at him in disbelief. They refused to let him return to London and brought him to their home in Rochester. An academic appointment quickly followed at the University of Rochester.

Mohsen was beginning to believe that in America you could be whatever you wanted to be. The saying was, "Go for it." No one criticized you for failing, but you would be disliked, mostly by yourself, if you never tried.

A year after going to Rochester, Mohsen realized he had to fit into the community of ethnic Germans, Italians and Jews. Naturally, there were divisions within the community, but the lines were beginning to blur, although there were few a rug merchants from Iran who did not appear to want to fit in. Other expatriates from Iran who were present were largely students escaping from the dreaded religious police. They were afraid to talk to anyone, lest there be reprisals against their families back home.

Khomeini's Islamic Republic was alive and well and eager to impose Sharia law on anyone it could reach.

The Administration in Washington adopted Saddam Hussein as a stalwart of democratic government and let the parties' blood let each other. Khomeini saw no problem in slaughtering innocent children whose only crime was the inability to commit religious dogma to rote memory. In any event, they would get sixty virgins in heaven. Martyrdom became an acceptable form of religious expression. It was also an excellent means of political control.

Mohsen decided it was time for him to change. With little notice and an absence of fanfare, he changed his name to Mose Ovasi and asked his friends to call him Mo. He passed easily for a swarthy Italian from Sardinia; never spoke of his background or his history and began to live the American dream.

At the hospital all of the nursing staff looked up to him because he was kind, always took the time to say hello, and displayed great medical knowledge. One day at the university library, he met Chris Webber. She hailed from West Virginia and was an assistant medical librarian.

In many ways she fit the stereotypical characteristics of what a librarian was supposed to look like. Yet, underneath her frumpy clothing, was a toned hard body. Her blond hair was pulled back in a pony tail and she wore oversized, red horn rimmed glasses.

With her southern speech and flirtatious social skills she could charm any man. She wasn't interested in any man, though, she wanted to catch the right man; she wanted a doctor. She would bide her time until one came along.

She liked to say, "My mamma told me to marry a professional man and he would always take care of me."

Mo was a target of opportunity and Chris knew what it took to catch such a man. It did not take much for her to snare Mo; a few nice words to a lonely, professional man and then grab him in the balls. When that was taken care of, she made her move.

One day, Mo found her crying in the employee lounge. Her makeup was smeared, her white blouse looked as if it were a towel drenched in water. He quickly attempted to comfort her, but her sobbing became hysterical. Placing his arm around her, they walked out of the building to his car. There was a deep belly moan coming from her.

"Chris, what's wrong? You have to tell me. Please, I want to help, let me help you."

Chris looked at him in apparent puzzlement, "No one can help me. It's all over."

"What do you mean?"

Chris knew she had to play her cards right or things would, indeed, be all over and she would have lost her chance for the good life. As she was the writer, producer, director and lead actress in an essentially one act play, she had to give it everything she had. Only Mo could determine if it was a hit, as he was the audience and, depending upon his reaction, Chris would get bouquets of flowers, or booed off the stage.

"You made me pregnant –I'm going to have an abortion. I can't live with this."

Mo was silent for a moment. Theoretically, he had no problem with abortion. As long as it was someone else's kid, he supported it. What difference did it make to him in theory? He certainly had no religious qualms about it. But this was a child of his loins, his flesh and blood; the grandchild of his parents. He could not allow this to happen.

"Chris, this is the best news I've had. I mean – like I am really excited. We are going to have a child. We need to get married. That's what people do."

Chris knew she had him hooked and all she had to do was reel him in. She wanted to be sure that the hook was not just set, but that it was set and counter sunk.

"Mo, I really do love you, but I don't want to force you into anything. I know you have your own life to live and I'm not part of it. A roll in the sack doesn't make a good foundation for a marriage."

This was more than Mo could stand.

"Chris, we are getting married. In fact, we're taking a flight to Vegas and are going to one of those little wedding chapels. It will be fun. We'll buy clothes and things there and have the time of our life. What do you say?"

Chris melted into Mo's arms. Six months later, when Mo was forty and Chris had just turned twenty-five, Wally came along. They named him Wally on his birth certificate. In honour of Mo's father, they called him Walid. Mo chose an Arabic name which meant "new born." But, for Mo, it was more than that. Walid was the name of his father and, for him, Chris had given birth to a new life in America.

CHAPTER 3

FOR JAKE, IT HAD been a long time since he'd been concerned about the threat of nuclear war with the Soviet Union. In fact, his concerns had ceased to exist. What was left of the Soviet Union was a dispirited Russian tiger, weighted down with nuclear missiles that would never be fired. Its politicians were only interested in leggy blonds draped in satin blue Sable fur coats, being chauffeured in black Mercedes limos, all the while drinking Stolichnaya shots in single gulps. The Russians didn't worry him.

Their politicians were as corrupt as our own. All they cared about were the perks of power. They would throw the crumbs out to their populace while the leadership continued to enjoy the golden headwaters.

What he really worried about were committed nationalists in Iran who had real purpose and direction and were fearless of the consequence; because they had nothing to lose. He always wondered if their social agenda would come face to face with his lifestyle, and send it into the toilet. It wasn't something that he thought about every day, but in the dark hours of the night he felt a tinge of anxiety when he considered the awful pronouncements that were coming out of Tehran.

* * * * *

IN TEHRAN, OVER THE last few years, radical changes had been taking place. There was an ongoing debate in the Islamic Revolutionary Guards Corps. Mahmoud Ahmadinejad had come to power and was brandishing missiles with the implied threat of arming them with nuclear warheads, just as Castro had done in 1960. The difference between Ahmadinejad and Castro was at once a dichotomy, with a chasm on one side and a seamless web on the other.

Both of them were ruthless politicians with nationalistic fervour, bent on creating a regional hegemony.

Castro sought to dominate South America by placing Russian missiles on Cuban soil and threatening the United States.

Ahmadinejad sought to develop nuclear weapons and indigenous missiles that could be launched against the United States, its European allies and Israel.

A debate was taking place in the young officer corps of the Revolutionary Guards. Castro had the backing of Moscow. Ahmadinejad only had the bones of children who were martyred in the useless conflagration with Saddam Hussein.

The Islamic state had ceased to exist as a theocracy as the theocracy had been overrun by the Revolutionary Guards who became the enforcers of national security. The IRGC controlled smuggling, the Straights of Hormuz, resistance operations and, of course, the diplomatic pouch.

* * * * *

MAHMOUD NEJAD ALIZADEL WAS a colonel in the IRGC. He was born after the revolution and studied history at Tehran University. He quickly recognized that his future was not as a teacher. He believed the only real course of advancement in the Islamic Republic was as a member of the Revolutionary Guards. Although he was not born until after the Revolution, he displayed a fanatical devotion to the teachings of Khomeini. His loyalty was never in doubt. He was a member of the young elite that would soon take over the reins of power in Iran.

Although it was contrary to Sharia law, he found fault with the concept that he who plays with dice is like the one who handles the flesh and blood of swine.

Friday evening was poker night and, as usual, he and his gang of five sat around the green felt covered table drinking Paddy's Irish whiskey and engaging in a game of chance. It was an opportunity to chill out from the business of the week. He had just won the last hand and was pulling his winnings to him.

"Mahmoud, you always win. I think you have magic," Firouz exclaimed.

Mahmoud stopped and looked at the officers seated around him. These men were his loyal lieutenants. While he trusted no one, he recognized this group as the best of the best and believed that, while he could not count on their loyalty to Islam, he could rely on their nationalistic fervour.

Everyone had had several shots of whiskey and there was a relaxed mood in the room.

Mahmoud thought to himself, *Allah help us if the religious police should find us now.*

Turning to Firouz he said, "My brother, I don't know if you appreciate our history and what we now have to accomplish."

Suddenly, all eyes in the room were riveted on him. The mood changed from casual and having a good time, to sombre. There was a sense that Mahmoud was about to say something that would impact all of them.

"You know," he said, "I've been doing a lot of thinking. The Revolution is dead and we have to change course."

The silence in the room was deafening. Mahmoud's words were seditious. Yet no one got up from his chair. Each sat as if transfixed and frozen in the moment.

Mahmoud went on, "We have to take control in the interest of Iran. It is not Islam that counts, but Iran. We are the oldest civilization in the world. For that matter, the only civilization in the world."

If what he said before was heresy, this was pure treason.

"I've been studying history," he continued.

"We've been raped by the great powers. Russia, Great Britain, the United States all promised that, at the end of the Second World War they would give us as much economic assistance as possible, because of the heavy demands made on us by their military operations during the war. They gave us nothing but revolution, bankruptcy and destruction."

"When Mohammed Mossadegh was in power and nationalized our oil industry and abolished the feudal agricultural sector, Allen Dulles brought about the fall of Mossadegh. He, along with the CIA, removed Mossadegh from power in 1953. He set up CIA operatives pretending to be socialists and threatened Muslim leaders with savage punishment if they opposed Mossadegh. It turned the religious community against Mossadegh. Mossadegh was a nationalist who would have led Iran to greatness, instead of this dead end of the Mullahs. Now we have to punish everyone for what was done to us."

Firouz was the first to respond, "But Mahmoud, we have Ahmadinejad and he is building rockets and taking us nuclear. The West is shitting in its pants."

Mahmoud thought for a minute before saying anything else. He knew this was his only chance to draw the others into his final circle. If he made one mistake, his life was over. He chose his words carefully, "Ahmadinejad is a buffoon. He can posture and make newspaper headlines all day, every day. The West and the Russians are not afraid of us because of his antics. If we were a real threat, they would simply nuke us into the Stone Age. We have to look beyond Ahmadinejad. We must corrupt the West so it becomes nothing more than a stinking drug infested corpse."

CHAPTER 4

ROCHESTER, NEW YORK WAS always a very provincial town. Ethnically it was made up of Germans, Irish, Italians and Jews. Skilled German optical craftsman found their way to the community as a source of cheap labour for Bausch & Lomb and Kodak.

Other ethnicities soon followed. Initially, there was substantial conflict between the Irish and Italians, because the former felt they held a monopoly on local Catholicism.

The advent of the ten year war in Viet Nam was a maturing process that brought the community together and established there was greater similarity than difference in the local populace. Being an American came to stand for more than historical ethnicity.

Wally had grown up in this sea of pluralism. Mo and Chris's friends always commented on the fact that he was so light, just like Chris. Mo would just silently say, *Thank God.*

As Wally matured into his teen years, he was extremely inquisitive. He took it upon himself to explore every nook and cranny of the family home, and was overjoyed when his parents were out for the evening. Their absence gave him the opportunity to pry into their private drawers and possessions.

It was a natural inquisitiveness, not prompted by any evil motive. Wally was simply a child trying to find himself in the restless sea of adolescence.

One evening when Mo and Chris were out, Wally opened Mo's desk and observed a large leather binder that was folded in upon it self. His natural curiosity gripped him. He snapped the button on the binder and opened it. Before his eyes he saw a one page document, "Certificate of Naturalization."

It recited the fact that his father had been born in Iran and that his birth name was Mohsen Ovasi. Wally's world started to spin out of control. He wondered to himself, *How could this be?* He had never heard of any Italians coming from Iran and, besides that, in school he had learned that almost all Iranians were Shia Muslims.

He ran to the mirror and looked at himself. He was light skinned like a northern Italian. He thought of himself as coming from the best of the Irish and Italian cultures.

Now the earth fell out from under him. It wasn't just that his father was not a native born American; his father was a Muslim pretending to be an Italian Catholic. He kept asking himself, *What does this make me? Who am I?*

Nothing made sense to him. He felt like he was not a real American. In school, he asked his civics teacher, "What kind of person is a real American?"

"I'm not sure Wally. We're a society of immigrants. We came from all over the world to America."

Wally was not satisfied and pressed his point.

"But Mrs. Johnson, whom do you really think is a real American?"

Mrs. Johnson could see that something was deeply troubling him. She thought to herself, *He's such a nice kid, I wonder why he's pressing this point?*

In a soft voice she explained, "The only real Americans are the ones with feather head-dresses, and the theory is that they migrated across the Bering Strait ten thousand years ago. So you see, we all come from somewhere else."

That did not calm Wally. As time went on, he became more and more angry. He was conflicted because he loved his parents and his school, but he wanted to confront his father and mother. He felt that he did not belong and would never belong in this society.

On his computer at home, he began to search for Islamic web sites in an attempt to find his place. He also began to develop an abiding hatred of the West and the spread of Christianity. The Jews be dammed, they were a minor problem. It was the Christians he despised. At the same time, he continued to go to school and excel in his classes.

Mentally, he was a deeply troubled adolescent in conflict over his identity. If only he were a dark skinned Arab, he would settle for that. He could not understand how his father had turned his back on five thousand years of culture, and thrived on the mendacity of the West. Wally longed to return to his roots.

The fact that he was the product of two cultures was lost on him. He began to view women as subservient to men and also decided that the Irish were primitive barbarians who spent the majority of their time in an intoxicated condition.

However unfair his characterizations were, as he approached early manhood, his beliefs began to harden and take on a mystical experience. He kept to himself, studied hard and tried to formulate a plan.

Wally's increasing self-doubt grew and he distanced himself from his parents. They perceived it as an adolescent stage.

When asked about what he did with his free time, like many teenagers, he would blow his parents off and simply tell them he was with friends. At the core of his being, he kept asking how Mo could abandon Islam for a Christian hypocrisy. It made no sense to him.

He began to believe that Islam was the solution to all of his problems. His home computer and the internet were his lifeline. His parents became increasingly concerned when he stopped dating.

"Mo, I'm really worried about Wally. He seems to have lost all interest in girls. Whenever I try and fix him up with the daughter of one of my girlfriends, he just begs off. I hope he isn't gay. I would just die if he was."

Mo listened attentively to everything that Chris told him. She was his pipeline to America and he trusted her judgment implicitly. Nonetheless, he did not engage in knee jerk reactions, and was not prone to believe anything about his son that might be considered negative.

"Chris, I think you're just overreacting. There's nothing wrong with Wally. I'm sure he has a healthy sexual interest just like any other boy his age. I can't conceive of my son as a gay person."

Chris was not moved. All she could think was that her son was going to turn into a Gaylord. To her southern way of thinking, that was the ultimate disaster.

In a shrill voice she exclaimed, "I don't care what you think. I want you to talk to him. I don't want him turning into a little faggot."

Mo was shocked by the aggressiveness and anger Chris expressed. He agreed to talk to Wally and see what was really going on.

A few days later, Chris was out with one of her girlfriends on a shopping spree and only Mo and Wally were in the house. Mo was in a reflective mood, seated near the roaring fireplace listening to the Brahms' First Symphony when Wally came into the room.

"So Wally what's going on with you and girls? I used to see so many around the house and now I don't see anyone."

Wally cocked his head to the side and elevated his chin, as he was looking down on his father.

"All the women I know are trashy and dress like whores."

Mo was in shock. He had grown accustomed to western dress and mannerisms. He wondered where Wally was coming up with such ideas, but merely concluded it was something Wally would grow out of.

Though they lived under the same roof and Wally ate at Mo and Chris's table, Wally's divergence had taken the critical step to differentiate him from not only his parents, but from the vast majority of Americans.

Wally was determined to lean Arabic so that he could study the Koran. He also resolved that his children would speak Farsi and they would live in their own country, as an Islamic State serving as a beacon to the rest of the Muslim world. He ordered the Rosetta Stone language modules and was on his way.

What disturbed him most was that the United States and Great Britain had invaded Iran and seized its oil fields during the Second World War. It did not matter that the seizure was to prevent Russia from collapsing into the Nazi Hegemony. He perceived the West's action as a crime against the Iranian people that resulted in the rise of the Shah and the repression of the Islamic movement. Good people had been physically injured and killed, as well as financially ruined by the actions of the West.

Wally was appalled at the materialistic nature of the West. He began to blame the problems of illiteracy, health, low cultural awareness and lack of modesty on the western beast.

He also came to believe that Allah was watching over each man and would judge him for every minute mistake he made. He understood the Quran and the Sunnah prohibited Muslims from waging wars for personal glories. It also prohibited killing of millions of innocent civilians in other countries to steal their wealth, lying to people, oppressing people, and committing atrocities against opponents.

At the same time, his personal hatred and sense of displacement overcame the teachings and he believed that the crimes of the West against Persian national sovereignty and dignity had to be addressed.

In his overall view of the world, discrimination against women, violence against innocent populations, commission of atrocities against opponents, and the use of Islam to gain political statute was not merely justifiable, but constituted a sense of national purpose that drove him.

His faith in Allah was subordinated to his sense of nationalism in the cause of Iran. He would do whatever it took to advance the cause. In the most fundamental sense he had become the conductor of the masked ball.

He was no longer content to accept Iran as a Third World country. After all, this was merely a term that was coined following the conclusion of the Second World War to describe the emergence of new geopolitical blocks of interest to the West.

Iran's problem was not that it was too traditional and needed to be saved by the progressive ways of the West. Modernization theory and western values did not pose a solution. Alcohol and drug abuse was not a Muslim problem. Alcohol had been banned in Iran since the 14th Century and America still spent billions every year to control alcohol and drugs. Everywhere western armies came, they left behind prostitution. Prostitution did not take hold in the Muslim world.

Wally began to believe that the Islamic Republic was the only solution. It not only assuaged his shallow religious views, but was the force to implement his political vision.

* * * * *

CHRIS CONTINUED TO WORRY about Wally's behaviour and the small part of himself he was willing to share. She and Mo discussed it constantly and began to refer to it as "the situation."

Finally, Chris decided that what Wally craved was a change of scenery. She told Mo they needed to move to California where it was sunny and beautiful, and where they could live on the beach.

She had already done her research and wanted to move to where Wally would be surrounded by young men and women who knew how to have fun. Mo was unsure that he wanted to completely uproot his life but, if Chris thought it would help Wally come out of himself, that's exactly what he would do.

In six months all the arrangements had been made and in the middle of Wally's senior year of high school, the family moved to Newport Beach, California. Chris and Mo had given Wally a chance to start a new life. He was eighteen years old.

CHAPTER 5

TREY STEWART FELT ROUGH hands pushing him into a little, windowless interrogation room.

From behind him, he heard a harsh voice, "Move it Stewart! I haven't got all day!"

They had taken away his shoe laces, causing him to stumble as he attempted to walk. He started to fall to the floor and was jerked back to a standing position. He could feel the strength of powerful hands holding him in place. He knew there was no escape.

He winced in pain from the grip on his biceps, "Hey, take it easy! I'm just trying to do what you guys want."

There was no release of the steel grip and he found himself shoved into a cold metal chair that looked like an object straight out of a Kafka novel.

Looking into the eyes of the two detectives facing him, he sensed a feeling of dread. Their faces were expressionless and bore no hint of warmth. Their eyes penetrated into what passed for his soul.

Trey was terrified for the first time in his life. He had lost control of his personal mobility. It was not that he had lost control of his future, he had no future. Cons in the joint didn't like baby killers; even they had a hierarchy of social values.

Trey was the lowest of the low; merely a speck of whale shit on the bottom of the ocean floor.

Time had ceased to have any meaning. Trey had been in custody now for seventy-nine hours. The Sheriff kept running him from local jail to local jail, depriving him of an attorney and frustrating the court's order that he be brought forward for a bail review hearing.

It was clear that the Sheriff didn't give a fuck what the court ordered. He was determined to frustrate the judicial process until he had a rock solid, video recorded confession from Trey.

"I want an attorney. I want to see my lawyer."

Trey repeated his demand over and over again but his voice fell on deaf ears.

Then a female detective came into the interrogation room.

Trey looked her over and felt a sense of relief. Women were always more reasonable than men. Maybe she would help him and do the right thing.

Looking at her face, he searched for a sense of kindness, possibly a friendly overture. She was an attractive woman of about thirty-five, and had worked as a patrol officer for some ten years before clawing her way up to detective.

Some of her colleagues talked behind her back and said she had made detective by flat backing it. They could not have been more wrong. She'd advanced through hard work, and was tough as nails. Her pleasant exterior was a mask that disarmed most macho defendants; Trey was no exception.

Noreen Taylor was not a person to fuck with, and Trey was no match for her.

She handed him a cup of black coffee, "Okay Trey, time to talk. You don't really want a lawyer. Do you know what's going to happen to you if we let you out into the general population of the jail? The other perps are going to pound the piss out of you. Then when they've inflicted enough pain to leave you senseless, they're going to cut your throat and let you bleed out."

Trey was speechless. It was worse than he could have imagined.

"What do you want?"

Cocking her head to the side, she paused as if in thought.

"I want the truth, nothing more, nothing less and you'd better be straight with me. If your not, I'm going to walk you out there into the general population. But before that, I'm going to put a jacket on you so they'll know you're not only a baby killer, but a snitch."

That was more than Trey could handle. He found himself talking for the next two and a half hours, going over every facet of the homicide.

Noreen was not taking any notes.

When he finished, she calmly asked, "Anything else?"

"No, I've told you everything."

Another uniform came into the interrogation room and whispered to Noreen. She nodded in assent.

"Trey, I want you to go with the deputy and do just what he says. Everything is going to be okay."

Trey slowly got up from the chair. He felt a burning urge to urinate and found himself being led to a locker room with a sink, a razor and a toilet.

The deputy watched his every movement.

He heard the deputy say, "All right, Trey, let's get you cleaned up so you look like a white man."

If Trey had been a black man, he would have taken great offence at the deputy's comments. As it was, he felt as if he had just met a friend. He was thankful to remove the stubble from his face and, even more, for the wash cloth he used to clear his eyes and freshen up.

Looking at his shirt, he observed the stains and wrinkles of having worn it for more than eighty hours.

The deputy sensed his distress and, as if anticipating it, exclaimed, "Don't worry. We've got a clean shirt for you. We treat people right."

Trey was thankful for the shirt and eagerly donned it.

"You're looking good, Trey. Let's go now!"

Trey was led into a plush conference room that seemed had a relaxed atmosphere. In the centre of the room there was a long walnut conference table with four chairs on either side. At one end of the room there was a single chair and, on its opposite side, there was an armed deputy standing next to a large video camera. Individual microphones lay on the table. Each had a little clip to attach the microphone to the speaker's shirt. Trey sat down opposite the video camera and waited.

Five minutes later Noreen entered the room and gave him a broad toothy smile. She assured him that the next thirty minutes would be a cakewalk. She just wanted to go over a few details about the homicide.

Trey felt relieved. The colour returned to his face. For the first time in three days he believed his life had been restored.

Noreen turned to the videographer, "Are we good to go?"

He gave her a thumb up in response. The camera was rolling.

"Mr. Stewart, I'm Detective Noreen Taylor with the Orange County Sheriff's Office. We met a few moments ago. I just wanted to reintroduce myself for the record. Is it okay if I call you Trey?"

Trey was really beginning to enjoy himself. This chick was hitting on him. All of his fears began to fade. He pictured himself walking out of the room and being a free man.

"Sure......whatever you like."

"Trey, for the record, have I advised you of your right to an attorney to represent you in this investigation?"

"Yes, you have."

"Do you want an attorney or do you feel that you just want to do this with me right now, without the assistance of an attorney?"

"No, I want to get this over with. Let's do it."

"You're sure of that?"

"Absolutely."

"I have some preliminary questions I have to ask you before we get into the facts of what happened. Has anyone made you any promise of what is going to happen if you co-operate with the Sheriff's office in this investigation?"

"No."

"Has anyone threatened you or any member of your family in order to gain your co-operation in this investigation?"

"No."

"Has anyone physically abused you in order to gain your co-operation in this investigation?"

"No."

"Are you giving us your co-operation because you want to do the right thing and get it off your chest?"

"That's exactly it."

"Do you understand that our conversation is being videotaped and that anything you say on this tape can be used against you in court of law?"

For a nanosecond, Trey sucked in a deep breath, considered what was being said and, without breaking his stance, said, "I do."

"Trey, you have a right to have an attorney represent you and be present throughout our interview. Are you willing to give up that right and proceed without an attorney?"

"Yup."

"Does that mean, yes?"

"Yes, of course."

CHAPTER 6

COLONEL MAHMOUD ALIZADEL HAD arranged to have himself assigned to a liaison project with his counterpart in the Syrian Military. As he exited the Iran Air flight at Damascus International Airport he marvelled at the diversity of people in the terminal.

There was construction going on and the scene appeared to be chaotic in contrast to the orderliness of Tehran's airport. He thought to himself, *Too many diverse people. Praise be to God that Iran does not have this problem.*

At about the same time, Imam Parvaiz had taken a Lufthansa flight from LAX to Berlin in anticipation of meeting with Mahmoud. In Berlin he caught a low cost German Air flight to Damascus.

It was easy to elude anyone who might be watching his movements because the Berlin Airport had over fourteen million visitors a year. Losing oneself merely involved a change of costume in the restroom. The flight into Damascus was uneventful.

Parvaiz hailed a taxi and proceeded to the Al-Madinah hotel. It was a previously agreed meeting place with Mahmoud and seemed to have a permanent Iranian presence on some floors of the hotel. Better yet, it featured Iranian television, which allowed guests to keep up with what was taking place back home.

Parvaiz marvelled at the clean features of his room and looked forward to a breakfast of Syrian white cheese with jams and breads. His stay, however short, would be good.

In the morning he went down for breakfast, taking a table for two. There were many families with children in the lounge. Spotting Mahmoud he made no motion to acknowledge him. Mahmoud looked around the lounge hesitantly, as if he were looking for a place to sit, and then walked over to Imam Parvaiz' table.

"May I join you for breakfast? There seems to be so little room."

Parvaiz looked up at him, "Of course. Please make yourself comfortable."

Neither man displayed any acknowledgment of knowing the other.

Parvaiz was an Imam but, at heart, he was a fervent nationalist. He and Mahmoud had known each other since childhood. Each had taken his own way in the interests of Iranian nationalism. They shared a common national purpose, and a mutual hatred of the West.

Mahmoud spoke in a quiet tone, "You know Parvaiz, that fool Ahmadinejad is going to take us all down. I think that he and the rest of the gang of religious zealots don't give a damn if the country roasts in the fire of a nuclear hell, so long as their religious beliefs are preserved."

"What do you mean?"

"Just what I said. A lot of the young officers in the IRGC want to replace the Mullahs. The problem is, the Mullahs hold the purse strings and it's hard to mount a counter revolution without money. We've been working on the problem for some time now and believed that we were on our way. Unfortunately, there has been a complication."

Parvaiz waited for more but there was just a stony silence. He needed to know what was happening, but was fearful of the knowledge he would acquire. Finally, he could not contain himself.

"Tell me. I want to know."

Mahmoud chose his words very carefully, "If I tell you more, there is no turning back from this point on.

Do you understand?"

Parvaiz felt a cold grip of fear. Nodding his head, he indicated his acknowledgement and acceptance of the ramifications of what he was yet to learn.

Mahmoud waited an instant before saying more, "You have to understand that there are traitors in every organization. Every man has his price. For some it's money, others women and, still others, drugs. You know we've been running a large drug ring in the United States. It brings us great sums of money from selling Afghan drugs. But a traitor threatens our whole existence."

Parvaiz felt himself begin to shake. Then he remembered Mahmoud's earlier admonition. It was too late to turn back.

"What do you want me to do?"

"Actually, we have disposed of the traitor but we believe he sent a jump disc to a Federal Court Judge as an insurance policy. The jump disc has all of the contacts of our operations in the U.S. He sent the disc before we were able to remove him. If the Judge should open the jump disc, it will be a disaster for us. Do you understand?"

Parvaiz immediately saw the gravity of the problem.

"What do you want me to do?"

"The jump disc must be retrieved."

He handed Parvaiz a small CD Rom.

"This CD contains all of the information you will need to act. Conclude your stay and take care of this matter."

Parvaiz finished his breakfast and made arrangements for his immediate return to the United States.

As he passed through Customs in New York he was worried that he might be stopped or, worse yet, searched and the CD discovered. Approaching the nearest Customs Officer, he saw that she was a young woman and appeared to be of Middle Eastern descent. She smiled at him and he could sense her treatment would be deferential.

"Did you have a good trip, Imam?"

"No, not really, I'm afraid. It was a very quick trip. Family problems, you know."

"Oh, I'm sorry to hear that. Do you have anything to declare?"

Shrugging his shoulders he responded, "No."

With that she wished him, "Good Day."

He was back on American soil. He knew there was little time to act and he would only have one chance.

CHAPTER 7

MY PRIVATE COM-LINE WAS blinking. Picking up the headset, I heard the distinct sound of Leslie's English accent.

Raised in a county just north of London, her speech manifested the pronunciation of the upper class that one would expect to hear on a BBC broadcast. Her phonetics and diction were perfect.

For me, she was a mask that disarmed most of my clients and adversaries. When they came to my office and actually made her acquaintance, they exhibited disbelief and pissed all over themselves.

Leslie was tall for a woman. She had high cheek bones with dark cat like eyes. He skin was as black as coal dust. Her parents had emigrated from Kenya as household servants to an English Lord and her voice and speech were branded by his Lordship's class.

She intrinsically knew the twin concepts of loyalty and discretion. Picking up the line she said, "Judge Thaddeus is holding for you."

I thought, *Oh, shit. I've forgotten about our lunch.*

Thaddeus Flowers was one of the few people who made it to the Federal bench without being a political whore. Most of the appointees got there by being politically correct and sucking up to the party big wigs.

Any state court judge who could pass the litmus test on abortion, with a record that showed he was a supporter of law enforcement and, of course, a strong financial contributor to the party in power, could become a Federal judge. Thad wasn't like that.

Some in the legal community said he was just a damn fine lawyer who believed there was some good in everyone, irrespective of ideology. Others called him a champion of the Bill of Rights, while a vocal minority was not so kind in their judgment. They referred to him as a traitor to family values and Christian culture; even espoused pulling him out of the courtroom and putting him against the wall.

The truth of the matter was that Thad had a strong Catholic upbringing. He liked to recount how the nuns would thrash him with a wooden ruler whenever he questioned church doctrine. Thad was an inquisitive man, beholden to none, who always sought an explanation for actions, regardless of whether there was a rational basis contained in the explanation. He would have made a great philosophy professor. Instead, he ended up buried in the never-ending cascade of drug case prosecutions.

"Thad, what's going on?"

"Not much kid. I just wanted to check with you to see if it's okay to go to lunch tomorrow instead of today."

"Anything you might need some help with?"

"I can't talk on this line. It's not secure."

"Alright ….. meet you tomorrow at the usual place and time."

Hanging up the phone, I wondered what was up. It was unusual for Thad to call me and not want to talk from the security of his Chambers. It was more puzzling that he did not want to broach the subject in our conversation.

CHAPTER 8

Lena HAD GROWN UP in the dichotomy of an ethnic minority, within an ethnic minority, surrounded by the Hispanic culture of Columbia. It was difficult to be a Muslim in a Catholic country. It was still more difficult to be a Syrian Shia in the Syrian Diaspora, where the majority of expatriates were Christians belonging to the Eastern Orthodox Church. She felt a sense of national historical identity with the Christian members of the Diaspora but, at her core, she knew she was drowning in a hostile religious environment.

In school she went by the name of Lena in order to pass more easily in the Columbian culture. Her brown eyes and pitch black hair allowed her to blend with the local people, without raising a shard of her ethnic heritage.

In Arabic her name meant tender. As she emerged into a young woman, she was anything but tender.

Columbia had a long history of welcoming Muslim refugees, dating back to the time of Christopher Columbus in 1492. In that year, the Catholic Monarchs of Spain decreed that any Muslims in Spain either had to convert to Catholicism or depart the country.

The beginnings of Lena's family in Columbia were shrouded in an ambiguous oral history. All that she really knew was that she was a member of a tiny religious minority and. while it was not necessary to profess herself a Catholic, if she were to keep her religious beliefs intact, she had to practice her religion in secret. To do otherwise would cause her to be suspect.

As a young woman she felt anger and alienation from the Columbian culture. Her aunt, who had married an American, sponsored her to go to the United States. She quickly passed the State Department background investigation and was admitted as a matter of family reunification. In the days preceding 9-11, government background investigations were superficial at best.

Having no job skills, she applied without hesitation for a janitorial position with the Federal Government. As jobs went, it was not one Americans eagerly embraced. Cleaning toilets and collecting other peoples' refuse was not an appealing occupation to the native born. It meant getting your hands dirty and the smell of cleaning solvents, instead of fine perfume, permeating your person.

Her workday began in the night and ended with the morning's rising sun. Lena was happy to have the job because it gave her a steady paycheck, and she was able to send money to her poverty stricken parents in Columbia.

Over time she proved herself to be a hard worker and became a supervisor assigned to the Federal Courthouse in Orange County.

Once a week, the forty year old Lena would call her mother in Bogotá. Their conversation always turned to the same thing.

"Ummu, I miss you so much. I worry about you all of the time. Do you need more money? Tell me and I will send it."

The connection was not good and Lena feared that something had happened to her mother when she heard only static on the line. Finally, she could make out her mother's voice, "Lena, I am an old woman and you should have been a bride many years ago. Who will take care of you when you are old? I won't be here forever and I fear you will be alone."

Lena convulsed inside. For many years she had felt the desperation of loneliness and isolation, but had always taken comfort in having a job where she could help her family. Family meant so much to her, but now the reality of age was eating away at her comfortable prison. She did not want a Christian man and, since coming to America, her eyes had opened to the contemptuous manner in which Muslim men treated their wives. The idea of being a mere sexual tool and baby factory for a man was contrary to the American way. At the same time, she craved acceptance and belonging within the confines of her ethnic heritage.

Life in America was different. In an effort at the appearance of pluralism, mosques sought the participation of both sexes. There were still high barriers to overcome, but the world was changing.

She took great delight in the preaching of Imam Parvaiz. To her, he was a humble and measured man, lacking the guile and arrogance of the Iranian Clergy. Her presence was not unnoticed. As a Shia of Syrian heritage, she felt an innate kinship with the Persian extraction of Imam Parvaiz. At first she felt uncomfortable conversing directly with such a pure man but, as time went on, she experienced a wave of comfort and pleasure from being in his presence.

Shortly after Parvaiz returned from Damascus he sought out Lena. When he saw her, he approached her after prayers, "Lena, I am happy to see you here so often."

"I love to come here ……..I take great comfort in your words."

"Tell me Lena, how do you regard yourself? I mean, you grew up in Columbia, now you live in America, yet you are a Shia."

In a second breath he added, "Who are you?"

Lena was silent for a moment. Confused thoughts came to her mind but, in a few moments, it was all clear to her.

"I am a Shia beyond anything else. I don't talk or think like an American – I always felt like I was a foreigner in Columbia."

Imam Parvaiz rejoiced within. He had not even had to bait the trap. Lena had taken the initiative and run with it. All that remained would be to reel her in.

"Lena let me tell you a story."

"The revolution has many enemies who dislike us. To put it another way, we have few friends. The revolution is in danger of faltering because there are traitors amongst us."

Parvaiz could see that he had scored a direct hit. He had only to give her instructions.

"There is a job for you to do. It is quite simple, but of great importance. You have access to the entire courthouse. We know that a traitor has given secret information to Judge Flowers at the Federal Court. The information is on a jump disc. It would be very embarrassing to our cause if the contents of that disc became public. You need to search the judge's chambers and can do that as a part of your daily cleaning ritual. Then, you must secure the jump disc and bring it to me. For you, it will be a cup of tea."

Lena was surprised by the request but did not consider it a difficult one. From cleaning his chambers, she personally knew Judge Flowers and was familiar with his habit of coming back to the Courthouse after eight in the evening, and working late. She had cleaned his toilet, mopped his floors and dusted his chambers so many times. She knew where he kept his valued items and also his handgun. She gave no thought to the consequences of what had been requested of her.

CHAPTER 9

GROWING UP ON A Louisiana dairy farm, sixty miles from New Orleans, was not a pleasant experience for Thad Flowers. He watched his parents toil from the dark hours of the early morning until the sunset of the day, only to repeat the cycle on the following day.

He was big for his age. By the time he was sixteen he was six foot four and weighed two-hundred and eighty pounds.

In the evening, the family would huddle around the Sylvania black and white TV and watch *Bonanza* or *The Rifleman*.

Their life was a far cry from the projected view of the TV western, but it was the only entertainment they could afford.

Life was a wheel; the mornings were filled with milking the hundred dairy cows in their tie stall barn, followed by feeding time. The afternoons were filled with calving and tending the crops used to feed the milk cows. The last chore of the day was the second milking of the cows at five in the evening.

Thad observed that farm life was gradually grinding his parents down. They had a weathered appearance, which came from hard physical labour in a harsh environment.

Still, in spite of their difficult lives, they had a sense of dignity not seen in most city people. On Sunday they would attend early Mass and intensely listen to the homily of the day. In spite of living in a poor parish, they did what they could to support the mission of the Church for those less fortunate.

Early on, Thad had exhibited an inquisitive mind. He wanted to know the origin of everything.

His father was not amused.

"Thad, you ask too many questions."

"But Poppa, I want to know everything."

His father's face appeared to have an intense strain clouding it. Slowly choosing his words he took the full measure of Thad, "Sometimes it's better not to know everything. What you don't know can't hurt you."

"But Poppa, you told me that when our family came over from France we were part of the nobility and had access to everything. Why can't it be like that again? Why does everything have to be so hard? I hate life here on the farm! It's boring. There's nothing to do and tomorrow is the same as yesterday."

His father thought to himself, *Yes, once our name was deFleur and we did live as aristocrats; how far we have fallen from grace. Now I shovel shit. The stink of the barn permeates every thread of my existence. Yet I have my dignity as a man. It's what I stand for as a man that defines my existence, not my title or biological past. How do I convey this to my son? I really don't know.*

For his part, Thad realized that, unless he did something to break this cycle of life, in another twenty years he too would be a shadow of a man and his life would simply follow the wheel.

Thad had two things going for him. He was big and he was smart.

In Louisiana, high school football was everything. It was the only ticket out of a life of rural poverty. No one had to motivate Thad. He played hard on the gridiron and also studied every moment of his time off the field. His friends used to tease him because he had no time for girls. He would mentally recant to himself that *'Girls are just hot plugs that liked babies. Get a girlfriend and you stay on the dairy farm.'*

In his senior year of high school, a scout from Louisiana State University was watching him play. Thad wasn't just big, he was fast and determined. It was clear he was a man who would never give up. A football scholarship accompanied him to LSU. When his college playing days were over, he elected not to go pro. He had higher ambitions.

He wanted to go to an Ivy League law school but the money just wasn't there. He also didn't have the right last name or Yankee pedigree, so he had to settle for LSU. Not that LSU was a bad school. It simply lacked the mystique of the Ivies. Any door that opened in his future would be because he made it open on his own. It wasn't that he was fearless, it was that he steeled himself to crave competition because that was his only way out.

On a chance interview, he snared a job as a briefing clerk to a newly appointed Justice at the 5th Circuit Court of Appeals in New Orleans. His fortunes were rapidly changing.

He began to look at life from the top down. Doors began to open and two of the silk stocking firms in New Orleans were courting him as a first year associate. He began to live in an ephemeral world of power, politics and money. Those at the top lived by their own set of rules, save one. Never expose yourself to public inspection or embarrassment. Reality could hammer a person down.

He'd been at the 5th Circuit for two years and, in all that time, he'd gone out to the farm only once to visit his parents.

One day, the Courthouse operator paged his line, "Thad, I think you had better take this call!"

Picking up the phone, Thad had an uneasy premonition that something bad was coming his way. Before he could speak, he heard, "Thad, its Mom."

He, of course, instantly recognized her voice, but the distinct tremor in her tone that carried across the line caused fear to rise in him.

"It's Poppa ....he's gone."

Thad sat there for a moment, not knowing what to say. All the good times he'd had in New Orleans flashed across his mind. In all of those times, he'd never thought to go home and visit his Mom and Pop. Now, he'd never get to finish his conversation with Poppa.

Thad had always been told grown men don't cry. But when a man lost his Pop, he became his Pop and the mantle of leadership passed to him.

He didn't want to be the leader because, to be a responsible leader, he would have to place the interest of others ahead of his own personal well being. It was the position that little boys aspired to and grown men run away from. Thad began to cry. He could feel the deep belly moan in his gut.

He went home to see his Mom. She didn't look like the Mom he remembered. She was withered and old before her time.

What had once been a beautiful woman with elastic skin was now a bag of bones with deeply arched lines in her face and neck. It was evidence of the harsh reality she lived. Yet, for all this, she displayed no rancour or anger. She was grateful for the time God had given her with her man, and nothing else much mattered.

They buried Poppa in the little cemetery next to the church. There was a large crowd of people who came to see him off.

There was no giant monument to celebrate Poppa's life, but, after all, his life was not made out of stone and false grandeur. His was the life of an aristocrat who lived as a common man and understood the foible of, "let them eat cake." Human dignity came from within, not from titles or the exercise of power.

By now, Thad knew it was time to pull up stakes and go to the mystical land of Orange County, California. There, in the sea of Spanish tile roofs and financial opportunity, anonymity could be maintained and roots were of no consequence.

CHAPTER 10

THAT EVENING WHEN LENA entered the Chambers of Judge Thaddeus Flowers he had not yet left. She found him seated by his desk.

He looked up at her, "Hello Lena, how are you doing?"

She nodded to the Judge and smiled, "I'm fine. Thank you for asking. If you need to work, I can come back later and do your Chambers."

"No, no, now is a good time. I'm going out for dinner and I'll be back in a few hours."

"Are you sure? I don't want to inconvenience you."

"Yes, go ahead."

With that he turned and left her standing with bucket and broom in hand.

Lena was a great fan of television crime shows as they provided an alternative to the mental stimulus that was lacking in her daily existence. But at that moment, she felt an incredible sense of excitement, as if she had been cast as a heroine in her own television production. What made it even better was that it was real. It was she who had been called upon to help overthrow the enemy of her people.

As she looked around the room, she attempted to spot the small black object she was searching for. Then she realized it could be anywhere.

She frantically began to open the drawers of the desk in search of her quarry. In the top right drawer she found the Judge's handgun. Picking it up, she marvelled at its weight and fine finish. She had been holding it for more than two minutes when she, suddenly, turned and saw the Judge standing only a few feet away from her.

"What's going on Lena?"

She didn't know what to say. Panic clawed at her gut and her life passed before her. Borrowing a scene from a crime show, she motioned for the Judge to come towards her and to sit down in his large black leather chair. Her moves were menacing. He quickly complied.

Lena could feel the electricity in her body. Her ears were ringing. She felt that her life was destroyed, but with the gun in her hand a sense of power came over her.

The Judge had barely sat down when she fired one shot to his head.

She suppressed her fear and used her cleaning tools to try and straighten up the mess. Yet, in the back of her mind she knew her deed would soon be discovered; she had to get out of there. She grabbed the Judge's calendar and bolted for the door.

Once outside, she reached into her pocket, took out her cell phone and called Imam Parvaiz.

He picked up on the second ring and she exclaimed, "There's been a terrible accident. I couldn't find the jump disc. But, the judge is dead. I took his calendar, but I don't know why."

Parvaiz thought to himself, *Fucking women, they can't do anything right.* He quickly directed her to a safe house.

CHAPTER 11

THE EVENING OF THE day Thad had called, I spent a long night with my friend, Jack Daniels. When morning came it seemed like a good idea to sleep in but by eleven-thirty I was moving down the road in the first Mercedes I'd bought in ten years. It was a gleaming black S-550 with a 518 horsepower AMG motor.

I needed a big a motor like a hole in the head but when I drove it I mentally regressed to when I was in law school, driving a thirteen year old hand-me-down Buick that used to belong to my parents. I vowed that someday I would drive the best and I didn't care what it cost. I asked for things and the universe listened.

For the last ten years I had been driving little sports cars, but it had become too difficult to bend down and get in. I think it was a combination of too much good food, arthritis and breaking the two hundred pound barrier. At six feet tall and pushing fifty, I could feel mid-life creeping up on me.

In any event, the Benz was a great compromise because it afforded me luxury and comfort as well as speed. I still liked to think that everyone was looking at me. There was no end to vanity.

I proceeded to Laguna Beach to the Hotel Ambiente. Driving down Pacific Coast Highway I could see the surfers on the beach moving with their boards into the waves. I gave little thought to the problem with Trey Stewart, and essentially dismissed the case from my mind because I thought it would pass.

The lot boy took my car and parked it four inches from the vehicle next to it. I could not figure how he squeezed out of the car, but that was the magic of being a lot boy. The hotel sat on the beach and had interior and exterior seating off the bar.

I was early enough to get a good exterior seat with a heater. The mornings were still chilly. I recognized the waiter as one of the surf bums who spent the winter on his board and the summer working at the hotel.

"How are you doing Bobbie?"

"Good, what can I get you?"

"I'm waiting for the Judge. As soon as he arrives we'll order something to eat, but in the meantime get me a double Tanqueray on the rocks."

I thought to myself, Life can be beautiful if you have money and time. Of course, you have to have good health to go with the money and time or it wasn't worth anything. I was lucky and I had it all, although I did have a couple of medical tests coming up. I decided that was something I wasn't going to think about just then.

I was on my third Tanqueray and found myself getting a little annoyed. Looking at my watch, I saw that it was almost one o'clock and Thad was still not here. I couldn't figure that out because you could normally set your watch by his punctuality. I flipped the cell phone out of my pocket. Actually, I kept the damn thing turned off most of the time as I hated it because it was a reminder that I was tethered to the real world.

I phoned Leslie. "I'm over at the hotel. Any calls?"

She started to say something and I could hear a different tone in her voice. It was the sound of fear. I could almost smell the fear over the phone line. Leslie was having a bad emotional reaction to something.

"Leslie, what's wrong? Tell me what happened."

The only response I got was some hard breathing and crying. Finally, in a very soft voice she said, "Judge Thaddeus is dead. He shot himself."

Now it was my turn to feel panic. I could not imagine Thad as a suicide; he loved life too much. I had a feeling something else was going on here, something that threatened the stability of my insular life, and I intended to get to the bottom of it.

I rushed over to the Ronald Regan Courthouse in Santa Ana. It was an imposing structure of granite and glass that looked strangely out of place in this town of minority immigrants. The building had been evacuated and U.S. Marshals with UZI assault rifles were posted at fifty foot intervals around it. I walked up to the security line and spoke to the first Marshall whose attention I could get.

"I'm attorney Jake Mandel. I want to know what's happened to my friend, Judge Flowers. He was supposed to meet me for lunch in Laguna."

"I'm sorry sir, but I can't give you any information. Give me your phone number and address, and I'm sure you'll be contacted."

For some reason, I found myself taking out my wallet and driver's license and watched as he meticulously copied the information to a small spiral pad. Walking away, I had the feeling I hadn't been as forceful as I should have been in the situation.

CHAPTER 12

THE SAFE HOUSE LOCATION was familiar to Lena. It was a typical 1950's cookie cutter, nondescript house that could be found in Santa Ana or Garden Grove. The house was located on the cul-de-sac of a wide street, reflecting an era when land was cheap. Large lots separated small houses that were surrounded by old trees, whose foliage kept peering eyes at bay.

Over the years, the neighbourhood had changed from a white middle class suburb to a mixture of Asian, Middle Eastern and African-American dwellers. Lena's handlers were indistinguishable from the adjoining home owners.

The neighbourhood was populated with people who had come from cultures that experienced negative encounters with public authority. They tended to keep to themselves.

The white constabulary was equally weary of venturing too far into the neighbourhood, avoiding it not only because of the language problems posed by the mixture of cultures, but also because of the explosive pronouncements of local activists in their continual rant against police brutality.

Save for its license plate, Lena's old car was indistinguishable from any of the other tired vehicles on the street. She pulled directly into the driveway and, clutching her keys, timidly tapped on the front door.

It seemed to her that an eternity passed before the door was opened. Stepping into the safe house, she observed two men. One approached her, took her keys and proceeded to park her car in the detached garage. The other ushered her into a dimly lit room. She could smell the stench of stale cigarette odour.

Lena was led to a small, rectangular table with a single wooden chair on one side and two on the other. She instinctively knew this was not going to be a pleasant session. With military precision, her interrogators debriefed her about the events of the evening. They went over it again and again, missing no detail. When she thought they were finished, she felt the tension in her body begin to ease.

Then she heard a voice from the far corner of the room. She hadn't realized that another person had entered.

"How long did you know Judge Flowers?"

Trying to match a face to the voice, she strained to see the man, but was unable to do.

"I really didn't know him – I just cleaned for him for many years. Sometimes he would talk to me when I was cleaning his chambers. But I don't know anything about him."

"What did you talk about?"

In an irritated tone, she exclaimed, "Nothing."

She heard the turning of pages in what she thought might be a book. Straining her eyes, she saw that it was the calendar she had taken from the Judge's chambers that was being examined.

"Who is Jake Mandel? Did you ever hear the Judge mention him?"

Lena had to think hard.

"I don't know him, but I remember the Judge told me I could clean early on Wednesdays because he always spent Wednesday evening with Jake Mandel. They were best friends."

The debriefing went on for several more hours. When her handlers were satisfied there was nothing more to obtain from her, she was led to a room with an old couch.

"You can rest for now."

Lena was grateful to put her head down and fell into a deep slumber.

CHAPTER 13

I FELT AS IF MY WORLD was rapidly falling apart. The two constants in my life were financial success and good friends. The practice afforded me financial achievement and I had a few people I could count on as friends. Now the success of the practice was being threatened by the act of Trey Stewart, one stupid kid who'd killed a baby. On top of that, my best friend was dead.

I wished I could turn to my wife and tell her the depth of my despair, but I knew she would only look at me and self-assuredly say, "I know you'll take care of everything." It was inconceivable to her that there was a problem I could not solve. But then, I couldn't expect more from her as her view of the world was myopic.

I had never formed many lasting attachments, save for the practice of law and my close bond to Thad and a very few other people. I could not count five friends on my fingers—not real friends who could be counted on in a crunch. The people I knew drank my booze and laughed at my jokes because they thought I had money, power or was important. That was a fucking sad commentary on the state of my life. I didn't know what to do.

The advice I would have given a well heeled client was, when you don't know what to do, you should do nothing. Personally, I could not adopt that mantra because I was somewhat of a man of action and decried passive acceptance of matters.

After a few drinks at my local watering hole, I finally decided the best thing I could do was to get naked with Silvie and let my essence flow into her. That was a polite way of saying the best thing to do was to fuck her and find some mindless slumber.

Silvie never caused me to question my personal assumptions and beliefs. I liked that because she opined there were no universal truths, just people trying to get through life. Who knew if she was right or wrong? What the hell did it matter? In another fifty years or so we would all be dust and no one would remember anyway.

In that optimistic vein, I found myself banging on her crimson red door. For a few moments I couldn't hear any sound coming from within her condo. I thought, maybe she's fucking someone else and was too busy for me and my machinations.

I pounded harder on the door. Eventually, I could hear the sound of footsteps. As her door partially opened, I peered inside to see who the other man was. Ya hoo! There was no other man, it was just my delusional paranoia.

As she stuck her head out the door, I pressed my face to her and gave the inside of her mouth a long motion with my tongue. I must have struck a nerve because I felt her mouth opening wide and she pulled me into her. My tongue played on the roof of her mouth. It felt like the original silk factory.

Our pheromones were raging. Sexual passion is the great replicator of the human race. Without passion the gene pool would simply die. As it was, neither of us required any encouragement from a rooting gallery. We were merely animals in heat looking for our next conquest.

I felt her wrap her legs around my waist and sensed the wetness of her panties as they rubbed against my abdomen. I could tell that her lips were becoming engorged with blood.

I liked Silvie. She was a screamer; she had passion. I was merely cerebral; a tool of sorts to satisfy her lust and need for belonging. As we wrestled down to the floor, the thin veneer of civilization evaporated in *ein augenblick*. We tore at each others clothes in a frenzy to mate.

Ours was not a shared sexual experience; it was an effort to achieve nirvana through oblivion of the soul. When it was over, we had not achieved a state of nirvana, we had achieved a point of rest. I fell into a deep sleep on the far side of the bed. I did not want anyone to touch me or offer me any spirits; I merely wanted to sleep.

At four-thirty in the morning, I felt Silvie playing with my dick again. There was no other way to say it. English has some words that are just self-expressive. I should have known this was coming. When you screwed around with a twenty-five year old child and you were forty-nine, there was no way to keep up.

I started to moan in my semi-conscious state but she simply said, "Jake, be quiet. I'll take care of everything."

It reminded me of the way women liked to hold baby boys up in the air and kiss them from their face to their toes. I wasn't an infant but it sure felt good. There must be something different in the sexual makeup of a woman that manifests itself in a different form of sexual expression. The only thing I could think of was they didn't have my parts as a man, and that this was the ultimate form of penis envy. What the hell, I laid back and enjoyed it.

CHAPTER 14

WHILE LENA SLEPT, A quiet, but heated, discussion was taking place between her interrogators and Imam Parvaiz.

"What do we do with her now? She is a liability and sooner or later they will track her down."

Parvaiz looked to her interrogators. Lena was of no further use to him. She had botched her assignment. The only useful thread that she had brought was the link to Jake Mandel.

Parvaiz carefully chose his words.

"She has to be placed beyond the reach of the Federal authorities. We cannot allow her to fall into the hands of the local police because, incompetent as they are, she could be easily turned to disclose what she knows. That would be disastrous for us. She is just a woman and no one will miss her."

Parvaiz' message was understood. With syringe in hand, Ali silently approached Lena. Pushing her face into the couch, he simultaneously drove the tip of the needle deep into the base of her neck and discharged its toxic mix of death. She died without a whimper.

Her body was quickly rolled into a moth invested carpet, loaded into her car and driven to an old railroad lot in Colton that was no longer used for commercial traffic.

Ali got out four jerry cans, each containing five gallons of gasoline. He bathed both the carpet containing her corpse and the vehicle in gas and casually flipped a match at the car. Then he and his subordinate departed the scene.

CHAPTER 15

WAKING UP IN THE morning and not remembering everything that had happened the night before was never fun. I felt light streaming in on my face and looked around; I was alone. I questioned my memory of the night's events and looked for my cell phone to see what time it was. Shit, it was almost one o'clock in the afternoon. I must have been really tired or hung over. I called Leslie on my office back line.

"Jake, where are you?"

"We've been looking all over for you. The world's upside down and you need to get your bloody ass over here."

"What's so urgent that it won't keep for a day?" I replied.

Then Leslie told me, although she knew I resented when she started giving me instructions. It was a control issue. She only had my interest at heart, but I was still angered when anyone told me what to do, regardless of their motive. Leslie was no exception. It was clear that I had to get to the office.

My clothing was scattered all over the room and I looked for my pants. But I only saw a few empty wine bottles. It must have been a hell of a night.

I finally walked into the office looking like a bag man from skid row in L.A. I knew the staff were looking at me but, what the fuck, I still had the corner office.

Leslie brought me a steaming hot cup of black coffee, along with a copy of the newspaper. Focusing on the print was a major job.

I finally managed to digest the lead story. It seemed that being a baby killer was not the only occupation of Charlie Stewart's son. According to the article, he was also a big time drug dealer. The Orange County Sheriff claimed Trey was not merely a bubble gum dealer in drugs, but a major player. I wondered to myself what office the Sheriff was really running for, and how he fit into the political puzzle of Orange County.

Brian Grady called another partnership meeting. Trey was beginning to get on our collective nerves.

There were five of us who were equity partners. The other partners had their names on the letterhead but, between all ten of them, their interest in the firm's assets only amounted to five percent.

Still being a partner was better than being an associate. Partners were harder to get rid of once their expiration date was up. Putting it another way, if a mid-level partner couldn't drag in new business and produce a hundred and fifty billable hours a month, he was toast.

Grady took a perverse delight in terminating them. It always came as a shock when a thirty-five year old mid-level litigator got the axe. At thirty-five, they knew just enough to be dangerous, but were too financially stretched to leave the firm and go out on their own.

When Grady would drop them on their heads you could see them implode. He always liked to do it to the WASPS. I never understood why the Irish had so much animosity for the Brit's. Their hatred and contempt just seemed boundless.

We affectionately called Grady the silver fox, although there was no question that he loved to get in the hen house. The worst thing you could do was let your wife or girlfriend dance with him. His charm was immense.

Looking around the room I saw Steve Kay, Eric Collins and Mike Spruance. Mike's physical features resembled his great grandfather who'd emigrated from China as a labourer on the railroad. In two successive generations the family had, effectively, merged into the

Caucasian population. There was nothing warm and fuzzy about Mike. He was purely cerebral.

Steve had picked up an eighteen year old chick on the beach in Hawaii. He had set her up in an apartment overlooking the ocean in Corona del Mar and was banging her on a regular basis. Leslie told me he hadn't been seen in Court for weeks. I guess young pussy kept him active.

It didn't much matter, because our machine was working. Toner and paper on one side, with mystical analysis that only a preacher could appreciate coming out the ass end, along with a statement for professional services.

Eric Collins was playing light housekeeping with a deputy U.S. Marshal. I found her to be an abrasive bitch. One of our corporate clients had a number of Lexus dealerships and Eric was always running cars through his business account for her. I hoped she could fuck better than she could drive but what the hell; taking one look at Eric's wife, I could understand what he saw in his squeeze.

CHAPTER 16

ENTERING THE MOSQUE, WALLY was struck by its simplicity and lack of ornate biblical artwork. It was stark, and had a feeling of emptiness. There were no portraits of any religious figures or statutes of people. On one of the walls he saw a painting of the great mosque in Mecca. The floor was covered in a decorative carpet with a repetitive pattern, and which seemed to represent a place for each worshiper.

In his mind, he contrasted the mosque with St. Mary's Church where he had worshiped so many times with his parents. In the mosque there was no statue of a man pinioned to a cross, with blood dripping from his wounds. The very architecture of St. Mary's inspired a sense of awe, with its high arches and stained glass windows. Its rows of hard wooden pews were a testament to the pain of the faithful.

In stark contrast, the mosque, with its simplicity offered no barrier between a man and his God. A sense of calm pervaded Wally. He did not know how to pray, but he thought to himself that the method was merely a mechanical act that he would acquire in time. In contrast to the men he saw in the mosque, with his white skin, he stood out like a red flag in front of a bull.

At first he was tempted to leave but, in a few seconds he saw a man approaching him with a broad smile on his face. The man wore a white knitted skull cap that covered part of his forehead and a white dress shirt that was open at the neck. Extending his right hand to Wally, he uttered, *"As-Salamu Alaykum."*

Wally's knowledge of the Arabic language was minor, but he understood the greeting to mean, "Peace to you." He had done a little homework before coming to the mosque and responded, *"Wa-Aleimum Aassalaam."*

Wally suspected the man was not Persian. In the Persian culture the customary greeting would have been to simply say, *"Salaam."* The man's ethnic identity was not clear to Wally, but at least he had taken the first step.

Breaking into English, Wally peered into the dark brown eyes of his new acquaintance. He saw the man's lips moving and a deep sound resonated from his mouth.

"I am Imam Parvaiz Samadi," he said. "How can I help you?"

Wally knew that his moment of decision had come. He had to carefully choose his words and express his intentions. It was now or never. He was on the verge of cutting the Gordian knot. He was still not sure if this was what he really wanted, or if it was merely a part of the maturation process going from adolescent transition to adulthood.

He stared back at Imam Parvaiz for a few moments, transfixed by the step he was about to take. In the back of his mind he knew that this was a journey of no return. Once he embarked upon it, his life would change in dramatic fashion. He was casting aside a life of privilege to become a simple pilgrim on the uncertain road to redemption. There was a dry feeling of cotton in his mouth as he felt the words spilling out, in a barely perceptible tone.

"I've come here to find my roots; I want to know who I am. I want to return to the Persian culture and embrace my heritage."

There was a look of disbelief on the face of Imam Parvaiz. Perhaps he wondered why a boy from a rich culture in America would want to throw away all of his material comforts, to return to the culture of his heritage.

His disbelief was coupled with suspicion that Wally was not what he appeared to be.

"Come to my study and we will talk."

He abruptly turned and walked to the hallway at the far side of the mosque.

Wally found himself following in quick order. The two of them entered an unadorned room. . Sitting down on pillows, Wally began to relax in the space of an educated man.

A servant soon brought tea and the mood changed to a conversation between old friends. Wally believed himself to be sitting in the presence of a holy man. He felt he was a man without guile, whose only interest in life was to follow the mandate of the Koran.

"It's okay Wally…..tell me why you have come."

"I'm not sure where to begin. My father is Persian and he's been passing himself off as Italian. I don't want to be an Italian or a Catholic. I want to be who I am and return to my roots."

Wally quickly related the story of his discovery, his inner conflict and his dismay with his father. In one sense he felt as if he was betraying his father but, at the same time, he knew he had to live his own life. His father had chosen what was good for him, but his father's choice did not work for Wally.

When Wally had come to the mosque, it had been mid-afternoon. Now the full moon sat low on the horizon. Feeling that his bladder was about to explode from the vast amount of tea he had consumed, Wally excused himself to go to the restroom. On his return, there were two other men in Parvaiz' study. They were engaged in an animated discussion in Farsi and Wally had no understanding of what was being said.

"Wally, I want you to come back for prayers so you can learn about your heritage. You can come whenever you want, you are always welcome here."

Over the following weeks, Wally became a regular worshiper, attending the mosque on a daily basis.

He took increasingly greater comfort in the serenity of the mosque and the egalitarian nature of the worship. It was as if each man had a personal relationship with the Almighty. Surely this was better than praying to a man nailed to a stick. It made sense to him, was linear and rational. He wondered how the infidels could continue to worship their false gods.

Wally found himself on the horns of a dilemma. The United States did not have diplomatic or consular relations with Iran. He wondered if he was a citizen of the Islamic Republic, since that was the heritage he had chosen.

Understanding that American citizens of Iranian origin were still considered by Iran to be Iranian citizens, he wondered if his father's status extended to him. He was also fearful of being deemed a convert to Catholicism and of potential prosecution by the Iranian authorities, should he return to Iran.

Wally had to prove himself to be a loyal Muslim subject of the Iranian revolution. He thought to himself, *I must be better than the average Iranian Muslim; I must show them all I am better.*

He quickly forgot his daily grammar school exercise of the Pledge of Allegiance. It was as if all of the years of recitation of defence of the flag and America had been relegated to the trash bin. With a single minded purpose he threw away his American heritage that embraced pluralism and western values for the xenophobic mentality of the Islamic Republic.

Imam Parvaiz was pleased with his student. Wally was a piece of un-moulded clay that could be shaped and fired in the cauldron of Allah's retribution on the West. He saw in Wally the potential to cause significant damage to the interests of the great Satan. Wally could pass close scrutiny, whereas someone of his physical appearance would be suspect. He had great plans for Wally.

"Imam Parvaiz I want to travel to Iran and see the Imam Ridha Mosque in Mashhad. I feel it's a sacred thing to do. I have to make the pilgrimage to Mashhad. Every good Muslim should do this."

Parvaiz paused to reflect on what Wally expressed.

"You have to understand that you have a higher mission. I know that every good Shia should visit Mashhad, but there is more to your life than a mere visit. You have to think about what will be the day after your visit."

"I don't know what you mean."

"You must understand that it is very difficult to travel to Iran. When you come back to America, you will arouse suspicion. The Americans will know you have been in Iran. You will be visible to them and will be questioned. We don't want that to occur. You are very valuable to the cause and we cannot waste you as a resource."

"I don't care what the Americans think. To hell with the Americans! I want to go home! I want to make my pilgrimage! It's my right as a Shia!"

Imam Parvaiz recognized that, while Wally was very bright and had the body of a man, he was still a juvenile. Perhaps it was from the indulgent manner of his upbringing. A child raised in Iran would have had greater street smarts, and would not feel that his caprice was superior to the cause. It would take more time to mould Wally into a useful tool.

"You have a mission …… when you are ready, I will tell you. For now you have to study and accept obedience to the cause. There is nothing more to discuss for now. *Il-Hamdu-Allah.*"

It was clear to Wally that he was dependent on Imam Parvaiz, if he was to have a future in his adopted homeland. He did not appreciate being rebuked, but he was smart enough to appreciate the words of the Imam.

CHAPTER 17

I STARTED ATTENDING AN evening class at Orange Coast Community College. It wasn't that I needed the credit; I was simply looking for something to occupy my mind as a diversion from my everyday contacts.

I had looked at the people around me and could only perceive a cesspool of greed and depravity. I truly was a part of the generation that saw self-satisfaction as the only fulfilling promise in life. In my own way, I kept looking for some elusive value that would allow me to transcend this mundane existence. Besides, I thought I might hear some new ideas, or have a chance meeting with a soul mate.

Life at the top was very lonely, the signature value of my existence. I found a class given by a young philosophy instructor; the ink on his PhD was barely dry. The class was supposed to involve an examination of the mind-brain relationship.

Dr. Gans began by asking the question, "Do any of you believe your mind can exist independently of your body or brain?"

A sea of hands were waving in the air. What passed for a response to his interrogatory was pure babble. A few religious people in the class took his question as an attack on God and the concept of creation.

I felt a sense of relief when they got up and walked out. Dr. Gans was quite animated when he began to talk and I actually started taking notes.

He said, "Life is never what it seems. The beauty of the industrial revolution was to create uniform predictable products that could be counted on to last for a specific design period."

"In the same manner in which we created products, stability and predictability was sought after in our institutions of government and our personal relations. The problem is that people are not machines and their conduct is unpredictable. Laws can be made to enforce commercial and social relationships; however, some individuals refuse to be bound by the rules and act outside of the existing social order. Violent criminals are persons of this type and their conduct is readily visible."

"Others who inhabit the corridors of wealth and power are not so easily detectable. Their lives are lived out behind high walls, some physical and others economic. The law does not address them because it is only the violent that the law seeks to contain. As long as such persons do not attack the perceived norms of the social contract they are at liberty to act at will . . ."

I felt my cell phone vibrating. Looking at the caller ID, I could tell it was a government office in Washington. I thought to myself, strange that they would have my number and why the hell are they calling me at eight-thirty in the evening?

I quickly answered and said, "Hold," as I exited the classroom. I was pissed that someone would call me when I was in my private time and, even more so, because it looked to be some moron in the government.

Out in the corridor, I spoke into the phone. "This is Jake Mandel. Who am I talking to?"

I could hear a female voice on the other end of the phone. It was a trifle muffled, but it had a distinct Ohio accent. I knew it was Ohio because of their way of clipping words and dropping their tones. I had a Cleveland girl once as a secretary and it took me six months to understand her speech. This one was no different but I caught what she was saying. I wondered what an Ohio girl was doing in DC. They usually didn't get far from Cleveland or wherever else it was they came from.

Eventually she was convinced that I was Jake Mandel.

"Mr. Mandel, I am sending you a package. When you receive it, do not open it in the presence of any other persons. The information is for your eyes only. You'll know what to do."

With that the line went dead. I tried to redial the number but only got an error message.

I wondered who was fucking with my mind now. Was this some kind of joke someone in the office was playing on me? I'd come to believe that life was not very mysterious, but something about this message made me uneasy.

CHAPTER 18

WALKING INTO THE HOSPITAL it occurred to me that my life was a fucking mess. I always seemed to be taking care of other people's problems and paid no heed to my own.

I found the grey walls of the hospital to have a flattening if not downright disturbing effect on my psyche. I had been here a month ago for a bone marrow test. My doctor thought I had developed multiple myeloma. A routine blood test revealed an M spike, causing me to go into a mental melt down. He re-ordered the tests and referred me to an oncologist.

I recalled representing Orange Hospital years ago. The problem was with some of their oncologists. They poisoned their patients and no one ever recovered, let alone survived. The hospital's morbidity rate went up so high they barely passed their JACO test. If the Joint Commission on Accreditation of Healthcare withdrew their accreditation, there wasn't a health insurance company this side of hell that would pay any of the bills the hospital submitted.

The best was when one of the head shrinkers came to me with their principal oncologist. They wanted me to form a professional corporation so that dying patients could have "proper" psychological counselling. It was no joke.

Now here I was going to see Dr. Death. I likened him to an auto mechanic working in the age of steam gages. Most of his work was intuitive and not rationally pursued. Depending on who you got as a doc, the life outcome could be radically different.

He looked at me with a flat affect and spoke in a monotone.

"You need a bone marrow test."

I mentally shuddered at the thought of it.

"What the hell. I hope you're a good mechanic."

Unfortunately, I had been online and watched the procedure. It was disgusting. Now I found myself back in the same hospital undergoing yet another procedure. This time it was a kidney biopsy.

I found myself starring at the radiologist.

"Give me a heavy does of the joy juice and wake me when it's over."

His response was terse, "Don't worry about a thing."

"It'll all be over before you know it."

The fentanyl did not take. I felt myself going into the CT scanner and the next thing I knew he stuck a guide into my back and inserted a nine inch needle.

"Hey, doc.…. I'm wide awake. I'm feeling everything you're doing."

He wasn't deterred and kept powering into me with his needle. The son of a bitch appeared to really enjoy his work. He pushed into my left kidney. Turning my head to the left, I watched him remove the core from the needle. At that point, I didn't know if this was a dream or reality.

"I've got to take two more cores, sir. Are you with me?"

Where the fuck did he believe I was? I was flat on my belly with a nurse on either side of me. I don't speak of the pain he caused. All I could think was that modern medicine sucked. The real article was not like it shows on sci-fi programs. Most of all, I wondered what the hell I was doing there? Why was I trying to save my worthless life? Was there a separation between mind and body or was that just a piece of fiction invented by men? I realized all I really wanted to do was to get better and return to the work I had done for so long.

I suddenly developed an admiration for the victims of physical torture—I didn't know the body had so many nerve endings. I looked at the doc out of the corner of my eye.

"Let's get this show over with."

CHAPTER 19

THE U.S. ATTORNEY'S OFFICE was notorious for hiring persons of Irish Catholic and WASP ethnicity. It had a small smattering of Jews but that was just for window dressing.

The real power in the office rested with the old guard. They were a bunch of wealthy carpet baggers whose families sent them to elite Ivy League schools and then turned them west. They always seemed to delight in telling native Californians that they hadn't got it right, but no need to worry; they would set things straight. It was as if they had a direct pipeline to God.

Their mission statement was to take on narcotic trafficking and put the bad guys away. If by chance there was a violation of a defendant's constitutional rights, no mind, because it was just about the good guys vs. the bad guys. So what if the law got bent a little along the way. After all, the United States should not be questioned.

* * * * *

AS SOON AS THAD'S death was announced, rumours began to fly in every direction. It wasn't unusual for the Feds to step in and take over the investigation of a death, but it was strange that such a tight security lid had been clamped down and no real information was leaking out.

I wasn't feeling great, but I knew I had to act. I buzzed Leslie. She came into my office not sensing my feeling of urgency.

"Call Jeb Price and get me the first available flight to Houston. Reserve a full sized car from Alamo and tell Jeb I'll meet him for drinks at Sergio's at eight."

"What if he can't make it?"

"Tell him this is a must do meeting and that I need his help. I'll explain everything when I see him."

"What about the partners' meeting this afternoon and the rest of your calendar?"

I was beginning to get a little short tempered. "Screw the partners' meeting and the clients."

She finally got the message that something was up.

I dropped my car off at valet parking at John Wayne Airport. A young kid was parking the cars. I put my keys and a fifty dollar bill in his hand, "Take care of my toy."

That was probably the biggest tip anyone had ever given him. He stepped all over his dick assuring me that my car would be waiting when I returned.

I got a Continental flight into George Bush International. I would have preferred to go into Houston Hobby because it was easier to meet Jeb, but all the cheap tickets on Southwest were sold out. I didn't care about the money; it was just a matter of convenience.

One thing about First Class, the airline kept the soda water coming. By the time we landed, I'd had four Tanquerays and was feeling no pain. I still had a burning urgency to talk to Jeb, but my stress level was coming down. I wasn't in great shape to fight the Houston traffic at rush hour, so I hailed a cab and proceeded to Sergio's.

Houston was never a pleasant place to drive, even in the best of conditions. The city was always repairing the fucking roads; I should say the same roads over and over again. Everything in Texas was bigger than anywhere else, including graft and corruption. Welcome to the Republic.

I had nothing to do but wait for Jeb. Sitting in the bar I casually observed the folks around me. Despite its traffic, I liked Houston. It had always been a real reflection of Americana. Unlike south Texas and Dallas, there were all kinds of people with different ethnicities in Houston. The people in Dallas said they smelled too many tacos in San Antonio. People in San Antonio reviled Dallas because it was famous for being lily white. Houston was just a melting pot.

Jeb moseyed into the bar and nodded to me. It was the recognition of old friends; we went back a long way. I knew I could trust him. After all, he was the only lawyer I'd ever known who had been an Eagle Scout. He still displayed his Eagle Scout certificate on his office wall, along with his other diplomas. He liked to say that after becoming an Eagle Scout, everything else was just going through the motions to get a union card so that he could practice law.

Growing up in Houston, Jeb had developed an offbeat Southern accent that he would emphasize when dealing with lawyers outside the Republic. It was disarming and tended to make Yankees feel like they were dealing with a Southern bumpkin. Nothing could have been further from the truth.

"Well counsellor, what brings you to these parts?"

Rather than beat around the bush, I came straight to the point, "Jeb, I've got a favour to ask you. I know you heard that Thad shot himself, but something's going on with the case that's really strange. I can't get any information. The Feds clamped down tight and nothing's leaking. Thad was my friend and I want to know what really happened."

I neglected to tell Jeb that I suspected Thad's death might have an impact on my practice and on the people whose patronage was important to me. There was no need to bring him into the drama. I could see from his facial expression he had a lot of questions. Jeb could be a gentleman or a prick, depending on who was the object of his questions.

In a very circumspect way, he said, "Why is Thad's death of such a burning interest to you? I mean, people kill themselves every day. What's different about this?"

I knew he wasn't buying into my explanation.

"Jeb listen, I can't tell you anymore than I've told you already. I'm asking you as a favour, to make inquiries in DC and get back to me ASAP."

I knew as the former head of the DOJ he could get me the information I requested.

I could feel the stress in my voice and I knew he could hear it; I also knew he would do it for me.

After two hours, Jeb dropped me at the Houston Hobby Airport and I caught the last flight back to Orange County.

I was seated in the back of the 737 waiting for take off, when the last passengers boarded. The flight was half empty. A very attractive, willowy blond of about thirty-five was walking toward the back of the plane. I could see the outline of her torso as she made her way down the aisle. I liked her blue skirt and white blouse. She carried a large black leather handbag over her shoulder.

Just then I remembered that when I was a kid, my mother told me never to talk to strangers. You didn't know who they were and, by chance, they could be predators. It was a good lesson for a kid, but being a forty-nine year old man, it didn't quite work for me.

Looking up at the woman I realized she had stopped at the row I was seated in. Our eyes met and locked for a moment. I'm not sure who smiled first, but the next thing I knew she'd moved into the empty seat next to me. I felt flattered and was getting a rush. My little head was doing my thinking.

Once she strapped in, I could feel the heat coming from her body. I knew I was losing it. I pressed the call button for the flight attendant and asked her to bring us two glasses of merlot.

Turning my head, I carefully examined the woman's face. I thought to myself, *wow, she's a looker.* I mentally undressed her and wondered what she really looked like up close and personal. She had a set of baby blues that made me feel like she was looking into my soul.

"So, what are you doing here?"

I wondered what her voice would sound like. I didn't have to wait very long.

"I'm going into Orange County on business and, hello, it's very nice to meet you too. I'm Aurilane."

Then she laughed and it sounded like music to me.

I was always a sucker for accents. Aurilane spoke like she'd just got off the boat from London. She had my full attention. My guard dropped and I could feel my dick penetrating through my underwear and rubbing against the zipper of my trousers.

I was completely taken by her and felt like we were old friends. I knew if you wanted to hustle a woman, you needed to get her to talk about herself. Yet, I broke all the rules; I felt I had to win her over and began rambling about myself and our firm, then I ordered another round of drinks and the time just seemed to float by. I don't know why, but I also found myself talking about Thad and my trip into Houston. I had completely forgotten the old adage of my childhood: "Loose lips sink ships."

The next thing I knew, the flight was over. We walked off the plane together as if we were young lovers on their honeymoon; until the time came for her to leave.

"Jake, it's been so nice. Sorry I have to go, but I have an early meeting."

She started to turn towards a waiting taxi.

I reached out and touched her arm.

"Aurilane let me take you where you need to go. It's no problem, my car is right here. I just don't want to let you go so soon."

I saw the hesitation in her and then a quick snap of the head. Her hair seemed to flow in the gentle breeze of the early morning and a twinkle came to her eyes.

"Okay," she said, as she extended her arm to me.

I could feel the excitement rising in me and realised I hadn't felt this sense of joy since I was about sixteen. I wondered if it was possible to be born again and have a second chance. I insisted on opening the door for her. It was a pleasure! It wasn't like being with a modern, liberated woman. I was with a woman who enjoyed the feminine prerogative and I could not wait to be her footman.

I parked in front of the Sheraton and walked to the desk with her.

With key pass in hand, she said, "I guess this is good night."

I wanted to make a pass at her, but suffered from the insecurities of a sixteen year old. I mumbled, "I'll call you in the morning."

CHAPTER 20

THE ORANGE COUNTY SUPERIOR Court in Santa Ana was built in 1967. At the time, it was a towering edifice that lent a quiet dignity to the local landscape. The architecture was thoroughly modern, in stark contract to the single story bungalows that dotted the surrounding streets. Now, Orange County was coming into its own. Soon it would no longer be a bedroom community of cheap housing for Los Angeles.

The courthouse served like a beacon, calling business and families to escape the riotous conduct following the Rodney King incident. High tech companies, professionals and law firms began a steady migration into Orange County; such migration upsetting the existing social order.

Population growth was also a factor that brought a demand for a new federal courthouse. Litigants and their champions were no longer content to make the long drive into downtown Los Angeles. Ground was broken for the new temple, the Ronald Regan Federal Building.

The old guard wanted it built in Newport Beach to reflect the location of power and influence in the County.

As if to penalize Orange County for its wealth and influence, the new Federal building was built in the heart of the barrio. Santa Ana was now composed of ninety-two percent Hispanic immigrants from all over Central and South America. Some were legal, most were not. The message was clear. The Federal Courthouse was plunked down in a place the local power elite felt inappropriate. Washington was only thinking about the vast supply of future voters that could be registered to retain the perks of the power.

Federalism was a powerful force, if used for what the locals perceived as good works. It could also be a yoke that controlled the local populace, without regard to its wants and needs. The infusion of the new courthouse created a tension level between the locals and the carpet baggers from Boston, who thought they knew how to manage the legal community better than the natives.

The Feds never did anything in a small way. There was no reason they should; they had the power of the purse. If there was something law enforcement needed and they could not pass it as a regular appropriation, the matter was simply tagged to a secret slush fund with a national security patch and the people paid for it. No one really knew what agencies lurked in the confines of the Federal Building. It was a fortress unto itself.

* * * * *

ON MY FIRST DAY BACK from Houston, a messenger delivered a package to the front desk of the office. It had my name on it and was labelled, "Personal and Confidential, To Be Opened by Addressee Only." That wasn't very unusual because clients often sent confidential mail in that manner. I didn't feel any urgency to deal with it. I assumed I would get to it in due time. Besides that, all I could think about was Aurilane.

By ten thirty my testosterone peak was beginning to level off. I found myself calling the Sheraton to talk to Aurilane.

"Good morning, this is the Sheraton. May I help you?"

"Yes," I said, "please connect me to Room 725."

"I'm sorry sir, but the guest is not answering. Would you like to leave a message?"

All sort of thoughts raced through my mind and I quickly said, "Yes. Please connect me to voice mail."

I found myself inviting her for a late lunch in Laguna Beach or wherever else she wanted to go. I was really getting silly. I concluded with, "Call me on my cell. I've got it with me and I'm waiting."

I didn't know what else to do. Well, that wasn't really the whole truth. I did do something. I rented a red 911 Porsche for the week. What the hell, you only live once.

Travelling down the Pacific Coast Highway, I watched the waves as they crashed into the sea wall. High overhead, I observed the sea birds looking for prey or any other opportunity to feed themselves. They appeared to have a strange affinity for civilization's garbage and could always be found near the dump, ingesting anything that was remotely edible. Their graceful aerial appearance camouflaged their true character. Perhaps that was the nature of life; a serene outer appearance, hiding the predator that lurked below. God, my thoughts were really dark.

I felt my cell phone vibrating and quickly grabbed it out of my pocket with a sense of anticipation of things to come. I was not disappointed. It was Aurilane.

I pulled into the parking lot at French Tide. In the old days it was known as the Friendly Breeze Inn but was converted to French Tide in 2010. It was a magnet for people from all over the world; the perfect lover's paradise. I hit the bar and waited for her. Two Tanquerays later I saw her silhouette as she walked into the bar. Her hair was pulled back and I could see multiple shades of blond and chestnut. She had a casual quality to her, as if she had just come off the tennis court. I took the full measure of her face. Her eyes were the colour of turquoise and widely spaced. Her facial features were what could be expected to be found in a Greek ruin. I just wanted to taste her; perhaps she would be the one to show me the way.

She saw me motion to her and walked to my table. I got up and fixed a chair for her. There were no words, we just smiled and stared at each other. It was as if there was a secret between us. I ordered a bottle of Pinot and each of us waited for the other to break the silence. I felt as if there was a tremendous chemical flux taking place. I was ready to pitch it all for her.

Lawyers always talk too much. I knew it was a mistake, but I started talking about myself, as I had on the plane. She seemed intent on knowing everything and I was a willing participant. Even though we'd been talking for a long time, I still didn't know much about her, save for her name. I just wanted to lick her skin and be up close and dirty with her. Somehow, along the way we started talking about politics and I said, "I think all politicians are whores."

"How so? That doesn't make sense to broad brush everyone like that. You're too smart to believe that kind of nonsense."

"You know, Aurilane, you're right."

I found myself agreeing with everything she said. I just wanted her to want me. Like any man, I would do whatever it took to capture her. I didn't know what the ultimate outcome would be and didn't care. It was the chase, the thrill, the rush; the promise of good things to come that excited me. She made me feel vibrant and alive.

"So Jake, tell me about your friends."

"Well, I really don't have many friends. I know a lot of people, but can only think of a few that I'd call friends. In my business, you just rub up against people and see little snapshots of who they are. After you've seen the snapshot, there's no enthusiasm to go back."

"Surely there must be a few people you're close to; a man or a woman that you're intimate with."

I understood she didn't necessarily mean physical, but still I felt a sense of hesitation. Finally, I heard myself saying, "my friend Thad committed suicide a short while ago. He was my closest friend."

"Was he ill?"

"Not that I know of. He just offed himself for no apparent reason."

"What kind of work did he do?"

"I didn't tell you? He was a Federal Judge."

Her look became more intense. I felt she was really reaching out to me.

"Was he working on something special?"

I thought that was an odd question because she didn't ask if he left a family, but I let it pass. After all, I'd met my dream woman.

"I don't know what he was working on. I guess it was just the usual drug cases. He never talked much about his cases. He was always very proper when it came to work, because he respected his position. Anyway, I don't want to talk anymore about it."

We got a room as the sun was setting on the Pacific. The light was broken by the louvers of the window facing the ocean. I pulled her to me and could feel the unbroken sheen of her skin.

She started to laugh and nipped at my ear. "Am I wet enough for you?"

I didn't know there are so many fucking positions.

When I woke in the morning, she was gone. No note, no belongings, nothing to hint of what had occurred the night before. I proceeded to the front desk.

"Good morning, Mr. Mandel."

"Same to you, sir," I smiled.

"By the way, the young lady I was with, do you know where she's gone?"

The front desk manager looked at me in a quizzical manner.

"At seven this morning, I ordered a taxi for her to John Wayne Airport. She seemed to be in a hurry and didn't say anything."

I returned to the room to look for a note, a trace, a fragment, something to tell me that the night before was real. There was nothing.

* * * * *

I'D RUN OUT OF clean underwear. There were two choices; stop by Fashion Island and buy some more or go home and clean up. I really did not have a home, although I'd had a house in Corona del Mar for the last ten years. It was a part of Newport Beach. In fact, it was the snooty part of Newport Beach. People who lived there thought their shit didn't stink.

Newport Beach had never been a very friendly place to minorities. In the 40's and 50's there were restrictive covenants in the land deeds that prohibited owners from selling their houses to Jews and Negroes. The Supreme Court finally made short shrift of that garbage.

I remembered the day KC Davis had come bursting into my office and exclaimed, "I've been researching a deed and you won't believe what I just found."

I looked at her very seriously and quietly said, "I bet you discovered that Jews and Blacks aren't allowed in Newport Beach."

I always enjoyed the look of astonishment on her face. KC was a sweet girl and a good transactional attorney. She would never be a litigator as she didn't have enough meanness in her.

KC had brought to mind what it was like when I first came to Orange County. After a short while, the presiding Judge out in West Court called me in and told me I was doing an excellent job as a Public Defender. I was really flattered. I did not know how to respond.

Then he said something I will never forget, "Mr. Mandel, I'd like to see you really go somewhere in this community, you have a lot of talent."

I still didn't know what to say and, after a minute of silence, he went on, "Mr. Mandel if you want to get somewhere in this town, you've got to belong to the right church."

I smiled and looked him squarely in the eyes.

"What church would that be, Judge?"

"Well ….. my church is a good place to start. The Episcopal Church is always a good place. It sort of bridges the gap and gets you straight with God and the community, if you know what I mean."

When I heard him speak, I felt a sense of rage. What a fucking hypocrite. I wondered what kind of objective justice he dispensed. I looked at him and began to smile, "Judge I appreciate your invitation and good intentions. But my people gave you a religion and I don't think you know how to take care of it. Have a good day."

With that I walked out of his chambers.

Pulling into the driveway of my home in Corona del Mar I found myself amused by my recollection. We indeed lived in a dark age, although so many people seemed to not know it.

In the late 60's and early 70's in Newport Beach, after sunset, we used to have NIN alerts from the police dispatcher. A lot of people didn't know what an NIN alert was. N stood for the "N" word. It literally meant, "Nigger in Newport." Not very nice, but today's generation had quickly forgotten their history. It only took one generation and memory was gone, although on the surface things really seemed to have changed. After all, I was a successful Jewish lawyer who lived in Corona del Mar. I wondered what the fuckers really said behind my back. I guess I didn't care because power was the colour of green and if you had green you could live anywhere. Everyone worshiped the God almighty dollar.

The garage door went up and I pulled in, parked and walked into the house. It was the maid's day off and the bitch was out shopping, I assumed. The only one who greeted me was my trusty bulldog, Winky. When he saw me, he ran to me and then abruptly turned around. I knew what he wanted me to do. I love bulldogs, but we really fucked with their genes. The poor dog couldn't scratch his own ass and he always had a terrible itch. I accommodated him.

As dogs went, Winky was no intellectual giant. He weighed eighty-five pounds and grunted when he ate. He also slept most of the day, periodically farting his way through the hours. I could always find him from the odour emanating from the room in question. When I worked at home, he liked to sit next to me. He smelled bad, but his character was good—actually it was better than most people I knew.

CHAPTER 21

I WENT BACK TO the office and heard a heated discussion taking place between Eric Collins and Brian Grady. Collins was an Orangeman and Grady was more Scottish than Irish, but passed for Irish. Collins had been brought up in the Church of England and Grady was raised by the nuns to hate all the roundheads. The fact they were such good personal friend, belied their fundamental differences of religious persuasion.

I'd never seen Collins heated up about anything other than pussy, and I was surprised at the intensity of his expression when I walked into the conference room.

Collins was sitting in a high back wooden conference chair and flailing his arms in the air. I could see he was worked up from the tenor of his voice. My first thought was, *Do I want any part of this?* Every instinct said no, but, then, I was curious.

It was lunchtime and the conference room was packed with the usual gang of brown baggers from the office. They were always willing to trash their brown bags if one of us popped for lunch, but none of the partners stood up to the plate and volunteered, so everyone had to endure Collins's rant.

He was a cop before he went to law school and was full of street smarts and savvy. I trusted his judgment because he knew how to survive in the hostile environment of the mean streets of South Central L.A.

Today, he was wound tight. He had his hand up in the air and was pointing one by one at everyone in the room. No one escaped his scrutiny. They all felt they had to eat his shit because it was not good form to ignore a senior partner.

"You people just don't get it.

There is a clear and present danger to our way of life and the whole western civilized world."

I'd never seen Eric this worked up before. He caught me off guard.

"The problem is that the fucking leadership in Washington just doesn't get it. What's the difference between Afghanistan, Pakistan and Yemen? Nothing! We're not in a war of terror; this is a war of global jihad. These fuckers want to kill every American and we just let them do as they will. They're a bunch of ticking time bombs and they're going to ruin this country. I'm also sick of the way American Presidents suck up to the Saudi family and bow to nomad warlords. I tell you people, things are going to go bad!"

That was about all that anyone in the room could take. What Collins was saying was just not politically correct and, besides, if we really faced a danger from violent Muslim extremists, the President would tell us. So far, he said that the extremists were just common criminals and we had no need to worry.

I walked over to Eric, "Come on, I'll buy you a drink. If you don't calm down you're going to blow a gasket."

"You know what Jake, I am so pissed. I see my country going down the shitter and no one is doing anything about it. Those whores in DC only care about getting re-elected. They just skim whatever lobbyist money they can get their hands on. I can't figure out what's happened to our sense of integrity."

I just shrugged.

"I don't know Eric. I guess we just got too big as a country and lost our way. No one seems to have an answer. I think maybe you have to make too many compromises to get to the top and, when you get there, the powers that be have the goods on you. So it's just a merry-go-round where the average guy gets screwed."

I knew my words were falling on deaf ears but at least he started to relax. A few drinks over at Paddy's Irish Pub and all would be okay again.

CHAPTER 22

IF GREEN WAS THE currency of America, white was the currency of Iran. Opium production and addiction had long been the favoured intoxicant of choice in the days preceding the Islamic Revolution.

The Revolution recognized that harsh measures were necessary to bring about a change in addictive popular behaviour. Stern measures were taken against sellers and users. Capital punishment was imposed at an unprecedented level. Rehabilitation centres were closed. The Revolution undertook a policy of zero tolerance.

Following the Russian invasion of Afghanistan, the Afghan economy fell apart. Poor farmers recognized their best cash crop was the production of opium. The leadership in Tehran shuddered because its efforts to eradicate drug addiction would soon be for nought. A gram of opium was cheaper than a shot of whiskey. The question of what was to be done about the drug problem was an issue that consumed the attention of the Ayatollahs. No matter how many men and women they hanged, the problem worsened. Drug abuse approached the levels of indulgence seen under the Shah.

Religion and money had always travelled together as good bedfellows. While the Ayatollahs sought to impress Iran with the customs of an eighth century value system, they were not against capitalism and exporting their drug problem to the despised West.

The benefits of technology were at their fingertips. Their madrassas produced an endless supply of young men willing to engage in the drug trade, if it would injure the West and produce profits for weapons research for Iran.

Quite by accident, the multi-headed serpent of drug entrepreneurs emerged. At first, they simply sold their destructive wares to Europe and eastern block countries. But, as time passed, the good news got out. Recognizing the profitability of its sons, the Revolutionary Guards slowly took over the drug business. In its zeal to corrupt the West, the hierarchy of Revolutionary Guards recognized that America would be forced to devote substantial resources to counter the effects of the drug trade. While here and there, men would be lost or imprisoned, it served the interest of the cause.

The net sum gain was substantial and the losses were negligible. With the precision of a military dress parade, the tentacles of Iran reached into the heart of America. Their conduct became a matter of national purpose. They viewed Americans as weak, ineffectual and unsophisticated in the exercise of power.

CHAPTER 23

I KNEW THE WORLD was mad and there was no order, especially when I got an e-mail from my nephew who was flying a King Air electronics warfare plane in Iraq. They cruised around unarmed, setting off telephone numbers hoping to explode IEDs.

In real life he was an airline pilot, but made the mistake of signing up with Uncle Sugar's reserve. What could I say? Kids were patriotic. They never saw that they were being used by the elites who ran the beltway.

The last time I was able to talk to John by phone, he told me, "Iraq is a shit hole and the people are savages. They had over five thousand years to move out of the place, but for whatever reason they chose to stay. They don't want democracy either. If they did they would have done something about it a long time ago."

I was worried about him. Hell, I was worried about everything.

Two days before he called, they had a rocket attack on the opposite side of his base. It was nothing big, but the rag heads managed to hit the shower trailer where three nurses were cleaning off the blood of the day. The nurses sustained minor concussions from the blast. There were a hundred guys who went in to get them out.

John had said, "Every woman under hundred and eighty pounds is starting to look good to me." I worried about his mental health.

In its infinite wisdom, the brass made it illegal for the opposite sex to be in another's trailer on base. What the fuck; didn't they understand a stop sign couldn't be imposed on human nature? A relaxing cocktail was also illegal. I guess that was the politically correct approach in Iraq's Muslim paradise. The brass couched it as an operational issue.

It sounded like it came straight down the pike from the White House. There were a lot of ways to bow for the sake of political appeasement.

✳ ✳ ✳ ✳ ✳

EVERYTHING STILL SEEMED TO be going wrong. Over the last few days, I felt like someone had been following me. It was an eerie kind of feeling. When I looked out of the corner of my eye, I had the mental impression that I was being watched. I couldn't imagine what anyone wanted from me. I keep thinking about Thad. His suicide just didn't make sense to me.

Looking in my mirror I noticed a black BMW three cars back. The driver's face was obscured by large sun glasses. After a time, it occurred to me that he was keeping a steady pace and seemed to turn off wherever I did. It must be a coincidence, I thought. Thad's death had made me paranoid.

I decided to speed up and lose him. My Benz has an AMG set of lungs with 518 horsepower. I slipped into the number one lane and saw the speedometer jump to a hundred and forty. To my dismay the BMW was matching me. I knew that something was very wrong.

I cut back into the flow of traffic and turned on the news from CNN. The commentator announced a news flash; that there had been an explosion in the financial district of Newport Beach. Details were sketchy, but one building had sustained major damage. The police and fire departments were evacuating the surrounding buildings.

I did a one-hundred-and-eighty degree turn and headed back to the office. When I was a block away, there were black and whites all over the place. I didn't think we had that many cops in the police department. Everything was tapped off with yellow tape and no one was allowed to approach the site of the explosion.

I recognized a patrolman who'd testified in a recent case I tried. I stopped the car and ran out to find what had happened. He was a nice kid. I could see in his eyes he now knew the face of death. His blue uniform was covered in ash and he looked like someone had just kicked him in the gut.

"Hey Officer Robinson. It's Jake Mandel," I called. "What happened?"

Robinson turned but didn't seem to recognize me. Never mind that I had grilled him with ruthless dispatch on the witness stand a few months ago. I thought I had given him an unforgettable experience.

It took a few seconds for him to focus and, when he did, his demeanour and voice lacked the assurance he had displayed at trial.

"Oh, Mr. Mandel, you don't want to go there. It's real bad, really bad."

I kept walking toward him.

"Come on kid, sit down. You look like you need some help."

Young men could be tough, but there was a certain crustiness that comes with age. I guess you learned to accept what was and simply ignored the emotional component.

We walked over to my car and I opened the back door, "Sit down; take it easy, everything's going to be okay."

I walked around to the right front passenger side of the car and reached into the glove box. I don't know why, but that's where I always kept a flask of brandy, in a shiny chrome container. I knew it was illegal but what the hell, I never worried about anyone searching my car. Besides that, when I went up to the snow, a shot of brandy always tasted good.

I handed him the flask and watched him take a shallow sip. Then, he took a long drink of the precious fluid. His composure appeared to be coming back.

"Mr. Mandel, I've just seen the most horrible thing I ever saw in my life."

From where my car was parked I could not get a good view of the street, but I hoped that our building was not involved.

I looked at the disbelief in Robinson's face.

"What caused the explosion?"

He had no response. I wondered if it could have been a natural gas leak, but couldn't conceive such a disaster. A lot of crazy thoughts were running through my head.

Then Robinson said, his voice barely a whisper, "There are body parts all over the street. I can't believe it; I fucking can't believe it."

I felt my hands begin to sweat, as a band seemed to constrict around my head. I knew I could not allow panic to overtake me, so wiped my hands on my slacks and touched Robinson gently on the shoulder. I needed to get his attention and to turn his focus outward.

"Robinson, you're a cop. Behave like one!"

He turned his head toward me and lifted his chin. That was what I wanted to see, although I doubted he could get up and walk away at that precise moment. But he was young, bright and I knew he would be okay. Just then though, I had more worrisome thoughts in my head. I began to question him as if he were on the stand, although much more gently.

He responded like he understood the game. He wanted to play; it would bring back the control he needed.

"Officer Robinson, do you know what buildings were involved in the explosion?"

"Only one building."

"Which one?"

"The National Bank Building."

When I heard that I became light headed. I must have begun to waver because Robinson grabbed my arm to steady me.

I thought to myself; do your job, Mandel!

It felt like a cold glass of water had been thrown in my face and I was grateful. Somehow, within the last few minutes Robinson and I had connected. We now shared a bond of friendship, as well as respect, although we hardly knew each other. If sanity ever returned, that was something I intended to change.

As if in silent agreement, we both turned our backs to my car and leaned against it.

"Please," I said, "tell me exactly what you know."

"It's not a hell of a lot. It looks like the bank on the first floor and the basement were hit the hardest. I don't have any official information, but I saw the damage and I'd guess someone planted a car bomb on the first level of the underground parking. I'd also guess that the car bomb was parked near the front of the street, but in the left corner. If it had been in the middle of the street, the whole building structure would have collapsed."

"How do you know that?"

"Well, I was in the Army before I became a cop. I was on an explosive ordinance disposal team and I think it's a good guess."

Now the panic began to once again rise in me. It was as if someone had jammed an icicle into my brain. I needed to know if anyone from my office was injured or dead. Fear ate away at my insides, but I still had to ask the question, "You said there are a lot of bodies. Do you know if the dead are mostly from the bank, or if there were deaths throughout the building?"

"I can't say for sure. The blast really shook everything up and most of the windows cracked. I even think some of the causalities are people who were just walking on the sidewalk. They got cut to shreds. But I don't know about the upper floors."

"The fire department got here in a minute and the fire started by the blast was put out really fast. I think it only got as far as the second floor and they stopped it there. Then they concentrated on hot spots. Now, they're doing search and rescue. I've seen them bring a few people from the second floor out on stretchers and a lot from the third. I don't think anyone on the first floor survived, but that's just my guess."

An uncomfortable look spread over Robinson's face.

I thought I knew what it was about.

"Hey, what you and I are discussing, at this very minute, never happened."

Robinson gave me an almost shy smile.

"You have an interest in the building; is that where you bank?"

"Hell, no," I said. I tried to smile back, but instead had to purse my lips as my eyes seemed to fill with tears. I took a few deep breaths and finally said, "That's where my office is; on the seventeenth floor."

Robinson wanted to respond, but didn't seem to know what to say. Then my phone rang. I pulled it out of my pocket and felt a sense of relief; the call was from Leslie. We spoke for a few minutes; just long enough for her to assure me that no-one in the office was seriously hurt. She told me that was in large part due to the newest associate, Robert Barry, who had been given the shit job of Emergency Co-ordinator.

Right after the bomb had exploded, power had been lost but the overhead sprinklers had started shooting water into the office. People started to panic, when out of the darkness and confusion a flashlight was turned on. Barry was holding it at waist level and shining it up onto his face. He was standing on a desk and while not everyone immediately noticed him, they did when he bellowed out over a battery powered mike.

"Attention mother-fuckers and bitches! And don't be turning away, because I am talking to you!"

With that, everybody shut up, although some crying could still be heard. Then Barry began to give out flashlights and orders, never moving from his spot on top of the desk, always keeping the light on his face. His orders were followed without question and, in less than seven minutes, it was confirmed there were no dead or badly injured, although there had been some trips and falls and some cuts from flying glass. These were quickly attended to and it had been confirmed was that the back stairways was clear.

Barry had begun sending parties down in groups of seven, because that was the best division of the flashlights. He was in the last group to evacuate the seventeenth floor. A lot of people were called heroes, but he really was one and, if he didn't get a big raise, there was going to be mutiny in the ranks.

While everyone got out safely, the water sprinklers had wreaked havoc on the machinery, files and paper documents. The general consensus was 'to hell with them'.

Leslie also told me that they were in a staging area for survivors, although Grady and Collins had taken a cab to a car rental agency. They were arranging for as many cars as they could get, for staff that didn't have alternate transportation. It was believed that, when the bomb had gone off, every car in the underground parking structure belonging to a member of the firm was totalled.

As far as the work went, Leslie had managed to grab an Office Roster, my Client List and her laptop before the evacuation. She wasn't sure if others had taken anything, but that was their worry. Having her laptop, meant she had a lot of my files available.

She'd also let the senior partners know that she had the Office Roster and would set up a phone tree before the night ended. Then she would contact each of them, each day for their instructions and any general information they wanted relayed to everyone in the office.

Beyond that, there was nothing else to say. She advised that I should not attempt to come to the staging area. It was chaotic. She told me to go home, fix myself a bucket of Tanquerays and be glad I was alive.

* * * * *

THE MORNING PAPER SAID it all; "Terrorist Attack in Newport Beach." What followed was a litany of injuries, deaths and damage. It almost sounded matter of fact.

It was as if the op. editor had had it canned and was only waiting to fill in the date, time and place. I wondered to myself what the hell was going on. Better yet, I wondered if this was a local grown malcontent who just went postal or one of the funny people bent on obtaining seventy virgins in the accelerated afterlife.

It really didn't make much difference to the people who were dead and injured. Motive would neither change nor heal their wounds. It was only important to the investigators who were bound to piece together, with methodical candour, the identities of the persons behind the bombing.

I suspected there were two tracts to the investigation. The local cops would pursue the matter as a crime, with all the blind alleys posed by a criminal investigation. The real investigation would be undertaken by the Feds. I believed they were the only ones who knew what the score was, and they weren't talking.

I'd seen enough black ops in my time in the army and knew that sometimes there was no accountability, because the operation was off the books.

In the back of my mind I started to wonder if this explosion had something to do with Thad's death. Things were not adding up, nothing made sense. I'd hit a dead end with Jeb and knew that I had to confide in someone about my suspicions, someone who was outside the loop. I needed a safety net.

I WAS BEGINNING TO feel more and more that I was under observation. There was nothing I could specifically articulate, other than having this weird feeling that I was being watched. I kept saying to myself, Mandel, get hold of yourself, you're getting paranoid.

I finally decided to visit an old bud of mine in Goose Creek. We'd been friends for many years in school and he was back in the States, after living the last ten years in the UK. Besides that, he was a federal firearms dealer and put together all manner of arms and people, primarily in the third world but also in Eastern Europe. I knew I could count on him for tools and information. He had his sources.

The biggest problem was to elude whoever was following me. I knew I was going to have to make tracks, but I needed to figure out how to disappear for a few days.

I hopped on the commuter train going down to San Diego. The train stopped at every little hamlet. I made a point of getting on the second car and as soon as the train was in motion, I walked to the last car. When the train stopped in Carlsbad, I looked around to see if anyone was getting off. At the last minute I jammed the door hard and jumped off the train. I gloated to myself, not bad for a man of forty-nine. I felt a certain pride in my body as I exited the train.

Whoever was following me would soon be thirty miles down the road with no ability to tag me for the next few days. I grabbed a vacant Yellow Cab and put a hundred dollar bill in the cabbie's hand.

"Carlsbad Airport and step on it," I said.

He swallowed the green without looking at me. I knew I was in a race against time.

Once we got to the airport, I directed the driver to a fixed base operator I used to fly from. I hoped the old owner of the FBO was still there. I remembered he had a Beech Duke he always wanted to charter out. Not exactly the fastest way to fly, but it would get me where I wanted to go in a reasonable time and there would be no record of my passage through any security checkpoints or terminals.

Upon my arrival, we quickly negotiated a price. I impressed on him the need for secrecy and added a little sauce to it by implying I was on a mission for the company.

A lot of the fixed based operators are conspiracy buffs and so my job was quite easy. It felt like the trip to Goose Creek had taken forever, but I knew my cover was good. Whoever was following me had to be frantic at this point, because I had just dropped out of sight.

The only difficult part was that I was only wearing the clothes on my back. No matter; I had a large wad of bills and was determined not to use my credit cards to tip anyone off as to where I was going or where I had been.

We literally dropped into the Charleston Airport and disappeared onto a taxiway to an obscure FBO. I gave the pilot an extra five hundred dollars and told him to wait for me for the next twenty-four hours. If I didn't return, he was to take off and go home.

People were funny and would do anything for green that never got recorded. Besides that, the pilot who'd taken my money he believed he was engaging in a clandestine matter of vital national security.

Argus picked me up in his ratty old VW. On the outside it looked like a rusty hulk. Underneath the bonnet it had an upgraded Porsche engine with enhanced steering and a sports suspension. Looks could be deceiving.

Argus was a study in contrast. I never really figured out how he sustained his lifestyle. By training, he was a lawyer with a Masters in Government but, for the last twenty years, he had not practiced law. He confined his activities to living on his yacht in the Adriatic Sea. Occasionally, he would go into the harbour in Tel Aviv and then migrate back to Athens. He always had good looking young chicks working on the boat.

Five years ago, I'd joined him in Greece for a while when I was doing a tour of the Greek Islands. I was in shock to see two twenty year olds crewing for him. It wasn't just that they were knockouts, they were bare ass naked. There was something about a lanky blond, twenty year old woman with a Russian accent that made my hips swing.

I wasn't any better or worse than any other man, but having grown up in our Victorian paradise, I appreciated a woman who had the body confidence to hoist a sail in front of two men while in the nude.

I only imagined what a romp in the hay with either one of them would be like. I suspected it would be anticlimactic because my anticipation was too high. Besides that, I thought myself too mature to be fucking around with children, although the temptation was there.

Argus was my friend of many years. In fact, he was the only person I had kept in continuous contact with since college. He'd eaten at my mother's table and knew my parents well. He was a great admirer of my father and his family. Perhaps he was the only one I could trust.

What I didn't learn until later was that Fort Jackson was the home of the army's Financial Management School. The army, like everything else was a business, and it was busy installing a revolutionary Web based business system called the General Fund Enterprise Business System. Financial management had become the critical component of modern warfare. If resources were not carefully managed, there would be inadequate allocation for future wars and mini conflicts. I had always suspected that Argus was connected in some way to Uncle Sugar, but I had no need to know specifics.

Rumour had it that his father had left him a large estate, but no one could live for twenty years without working. I guess if I pencilled in the dots, I would have connected the point that as a Federal Fire Arms Dealer, he had to have government sanction to operate. That coupled to his activities in the Balkans and Middle East, allowed a clearer picture to emerge.

I didn't know what help he could give me, but I was beginning to suspect something was radically wrong and could not figure out where all the pieces fit together.

At six foot four, he towered over my six foot frame. I was big and heavily muscled, but he was the extra large size.

He grabbed me in a bear hug.

"Jake I'm so happy you're here. You look like you've seen a ghost. What's wrong?"

We got into the car and started driving away.

"I'm not sure where to begin."

"You remember me telling you about my friend, Thad?"

"Yeah, he's the good guy that became a Federal judge."

"Well, he's dead. The Feds say he shot himself, but I don't believe it. It just doesn't make sense."

Argus was quiet for a moment. I could hear the drone of the VW's motor as we sped down the road.

Finally he said, "Have any other unusual things been happening in your life?"

That struck me as an odd question. I rapidly told him I was afraid someone was following me and about the explosion at our office building. I took care to detail how I had managed come to him and that I believed I had effectively dropped from sight.

A few minutes later, he pulled off onto a dirt road and parked the VW behind some trees. We were screened from the road and the trees were dense enough to screen us from the air. A deep frown came over his face. I could see that he was carefully thinking about what he should tell me.

Finally, he said, "Jake, you need to get out of here. You're into something you don't want any part of. I don't want anyone to know that you've been around." With that he turned the VW around and started back to the FBO.

At first there was a stony silence but, after a few minutes he said, "Listen to me. You're in a lot of danger. I don't know who the exact players are, but I'm going to look around and see what I can find out. In the meantime, don't trust anyone. Nothing is as it seems."

He handed me a small piece of paper.

"This is a private number where you can reach me. Don't call me from your cell phone. Don't use your office phone or home phone. If you need to reach me, call from a public phone. This number doesn't show up in any government data base, but I can never be 100% certain. Keep your calls under fifty-eight seconds."

He added, "For your own protection, I'm going to send you some weapons and explosives. The guns have no serial markings and can't be traced. Stash them in strategic places. The explosives look harmless. They actually contain high grade Semtex. I don't know if you'll need them, but it's better to be prepared."

"What the hell are you talking about?"

His comments and sudden about turn completely bewildered me. I hadn't fired a weapon since my days in Bosnia.

"Jake, listen to me. If what I suspect is true, you're in a hell of a lot of danger. No one is going to come to your rescue. You're going to have to protect yourself. And don't bring the cops in! This is way above their pay grade. I'll be in touch with you; I'll know how to find you when I know more."

With that, he dropped me in front of the FBO and sped off into the darkness.

CHAPTER 24

THE PILOT OF THE Beech Duke was still waiting for me. The old adage was true; money talks, people listen.

He'd filled his tanks in anticipation of our return flight. I grabbed a couple of sandwiches from the vending machine and two bottles of Coke. It was going to be a long night.

As we walked over to the tie down where the plane was anchored, he said, "Where are we going now?"

"I'll let you know when we do the pre-flight run-up."

As he was doing his run-up, I was thinking about what to do. I didn't want to file a flight plan on the chance that whoever was following me might locate us.

The run-up was complete.

"All right this is what I want you to do. First of all, file no flight plan! Ask the tower for a Visual Flight Rules release and then tell them we're just going for a spin around the neighbourhood. Once we get airborne, the tower's going to want to hand you off to Air Traffic Control. But, before they do that, I want you to kill your transponder and get down to a hundred feet above ground level. We're just going to disappear by flying due west, and then we'll switch our course north and land at Willow Municipal Airport in Detroit."

The pilot's face turned white. I could tell he was afraid that he was getting in over his head. Shutting down a transponder was a license event, but five Ben Franklins and my assurance that this mission had been sanctioned at the highest level, helped him to regain his confidence.

I was amazed at the bullshit people would buy into and the small amount of grease it took to gain their co-operation.

Willow was basically a general aviation airport with a large freight operation. No one gave a shit who came and went. We slipped quietly into the airport. I paid the pilot and told him this was where I permanently got off and the trip ended.

Then I made my way over to Nordstrom's and got a change of clothes. I like Hickey-Freeman suits. They make a statement. The clerk was happy to ring me up as I'd just spent seventeen hundred dollars on a suit, tie and shirt. I couldn't believe it, but the whole outfit looked like it had been cut just for me. The pants and jacket fit perfectly.

Looking at the clerk, I said, "I'll just wear this for now. Put my old clothes in a bag and I'll take them with me."

There was a look of surprise on her face, but a smile from me quickly disarmed her.

I was starting to run low on cash, so I had her look up my credit card account number. Everything checked out and, as I was at the other end of the world from Argus, I felt I had dodged the bullet and could go back to Newport Beach. No one would ever know where I had been or what my mission was.

I took the bag with me and, as I walked out to catch a hack to the Detroit Airport, I came upon a homeless man standing on the sidewalk. He was about my height and weight. I just handed him the bag of clothes. He must have been on the street for a long time, because he did not seem to have the ability to look directly into my eyes. He just took the bag and kept on walking.

My trip out of Detroit was interesting. I bought a First Class one way ticket to L.A. The gate agent was a little suspicious because of the one way flight, and the fact that I was travelling without luggage.

I walked up to security and handed the boarding pass to the moron from TSA. He was actually an eighth grade drop- out who probably used to be a baggage handler working for minimum wage. No need for concern. The government had given him a blue uniform and gold badge and he was suddenly anointed with wisdom and discretion. He looked at the 9T on my boarding pass. I hadn't even noticed it. Shit, it was a security alert.

"Sir, come with me please."

He got up from his chair and shut the whole line down. People behind me were pissed. We walked over to another station and he proceeded to carry on a conversation with the man in charge.

The next thing I knew, I was being interrogated as to why I was taking a one way flight to L.A. I was beginning to get a little hostile. I was fed up with government bureaucrats who thought it was their duty to violate my right of free passage and privacy, all in the name of public safety.

I said to myself, *fucking Arabs; it isn't bad enough that they rob us every day at the gas pump, but now they've fucked up our whole country and ruined our transportation system.* I felt like shouting it out, but then some politically correct left winger would accuse me of being a racist. I was so tired of what I felt they'd done to our country. I was not a one worlder, but I recognized evil when I saw it.

"Step over here, sir!" a security official called out to me.

I looked to where he wanted me to go. It was a sealed transparent chamber with gas jets. It did not make me feel comfortable. I walked into the chamber and felt the door click behind me. The next thing I knew, there was hissing and puff of air being thrown at me.

When it was over I asked him, "What the fuck was that all about?"

The Transportation Security Administration guy looked at me with a sly grin and said, "Checking for chemical explosives on your person. Please proceed to your gate."

CHAPTER 25

I TOOK THE AIRPORT train down to gate A78 at the end of the terminal.

Having two hours to kill, I walked over to the newsstand and bought a Detroit Free Press and a tall cup of coffee at Starbucks.

There were two newspapers I enjoyed reading; The Atlanta Journal Constitution and The Detroit Free Press. They both told it like it was, without homogenizing the message.

I didn't know where they found their reporters. They were two cuts above CNN and had no political agenda. It was a pleasure to read facts without the reporter's political views becoming a part of the story. So much of what passed for news was just wagging heads and political rhetoric. It was comforting to know that at least in the Midwest and South, journalists still had some modicum of integrity.

When I thought about it, it occurred to me that this was a novel concept given the manner in which the news was managed by the elites. I wasn't a populist but I just wanted the unvarnished version of what was happening in our daily lives. That didn't seem too much to expect but I'd begun to believe it was. Perhaps the independents were right and there wasn't a nickel's worth of difference between the Dems and Republicans, but I'd sure hate to lose my faith in the political process.

As if to wake me out of my thoughts, an announcement came over the public address system. "All confirmed passengers on Delta Flight 2358; we will begin boarding in five minutes."

Suddenly, most of the passengers in the terminal woke up and crowded around the gate. I could not figure out why they were pushing.

Delta was pretty good about boarding First Class and then by zones, but some people felt they always had to be at the head of the line. It didn't matter that the line was not going anywhere; they just had to be first.

As I walked into the Airbus, I started to sit down in seat 2A. A flight attendant took my jacket.

"What would you like to drink, Sir?"

I looked her over and, in an instant concluded, so much for unionization. She was hitting forty-five and her blond hair was splintered. I'm sure she was attractive in the days when she had been called a stewardess. But now she was just one more matronly flight attendant, who was working so that she and her husband could have pass privileges on the airline.

I liked it better when a perky stewardess would walk up to me and say, "Coffee, tea or me?" That was the male chauvinist in me. While I might be sorry if that pissed off a feminist here and there, a man was what a man did and I liked my girls, not women, young and sassy.

"Sweetie," I said, "Get me a couple of bottles of Jack with some ice."

In an instant she was gone and I flopped into my seat. I hadn't realize how mentally exhausted I was.

I picked up my Detroit Free Press and began to read. In a few minutes I had downed the Jack and was sucking the last taste of the bourbon off the ice cubes. There was an interesting story focusing on the Dearborn suburbs.

It seemed that Dearborn was becoming the Mecca for Arab Americans in their migration to the United States. I thought it was good to have a new immigrant population, because it had been the successive waves of immigrants that had made this country great.

As I continued to read the story, immigration was only the tip of the report. The reporter was saying that Dearborn now had thirty thousand Arab Americans and they had brought their culture and traditions here. I thought, *that's good, it'll enrich all of us.* However, there was a dark side to the article. A father from Egypt was angered by his daughters. I understood that; daughters could be a pain in the ass. They were sometimes rebellious and really nasty in their teen years. One of my partners was fond of saying, "Daughters are trouble until they have their own kids. Then they suddenly realize what nice people their parents are." I'm not sure if he was correct, but the thought popped into my mind.

What was interesting to me was how the father handled his anger. He'd murdered his two daughters. In a note to his wife he'd said it was an "Honour Killing", because they had become westernized and were going out with Christians. That really caught my attention.

I wondered what the fuck is an "Honour Killing" was and how killing a child could be justified, just because she went out with someone from a different religious background. How was the family shamed? What did the family have to do with it? It was the daughters' choice who they wanted to date. It didn't make much sense to me.

I guess I was deeply absorbed in the article, because I didn't pay any attention to the man who sat down beside me in 2B. I preferred my own company on a flight and really resented it when I got a chatty Kathy sitting next to me. Not that the guy did anything to me; I just wanted my space.

I could hear him talking and it suddenly occurred to me that to not respond would be a total social gaff. Turning to him I said, "Sorry, I didn't get what you were saying."

That seemed to be all the encouragement he required. "How did you like Detroit?"

I'd learned it was better to listen than to give anything away, so I just smiled and nodded.

"It was good."

"Well, I was here visiting my relatives who moved here from Ramallah."

I wasn't quite sure where Ramallah was so I again smiled and nodded. That was all the encouragement he seemed to need.

"They are doing quite good in America. It's too bad they had to leave Palestine. It's always hard to be an immigrant in a strange land. I see you were reading about Detroit. Nasty business what's going on there."

I couldn't figure out who or what this guy was. He appeared to be well dressed and was wearing expensive eyeglasses. I guessed his glasses cost as much as my suit. He had a pinkie diamond that was at least three carats. I watched it as he waived his hands in an animated fashion as he spoke.

Then I decided it would be fun to interview him and dropped into my lawyer role.

"So where do you come from?"

"I'm from Palestine."

I looked at him quizzically, "I don't know any country called Palestine. What city are you from?"

He explained that he came from Akko, an Arab town in Israel.

"So you're an Israeli," I said.

His response was visceral.

"Never. Never, *Imshalem!*"

I don't understand. Isn't Akko a part of Israel?

What kind of passport are you travelling on?" I could see that I had touched a raw nerve.

"You know the Jews are no good. They don't care when an Arab is murdered by an Arab. They don't enforce the law and criminals know that their chance of being caught and punished is nil. There is so much violence in our community. It has to be stopped. It is immoral and illegal what's going on. The Arab minority has to be protected and that's not being done."

My initial reaction was that this was a very concerned man. Perhaps it would be interesting to engage him for the next four hours of flight.

"So how do you feel about Arab terrorists murdering Jewish Israelis?"

Before he could answer I found myself asking another question.

"……And what are your thoughts about Arabs murdering Jewish Israeli children in the name of resistance?"

A pained look came over his face. I felt I had met a righteous man; a man of principal and conviction.

He smiled and seemed to puff up with pride.

"I think that Arabs who are convicted of murdering Israelis or of involvement in terrorist attacks are prisoners of freedom. They must be released immediately, along with all the other Palestinian prisoners."

He appeared to be an educated man, but I could not understand his logic.

"Tell me something, how can you release murderers of Jewish children? Shouldn't they be punished the same way as murderers of Arab children?"

He looked at me in exasperation, "You don't get it. Who cares about the Jews? They are just vermin. They are not entitled to the same consideration as Arab victims."

I turned in my seat and waited for the time to pass. I felt like I was sitting next to a leper. This man carried a vile, loathsome disease. No matter how many books he'd read or how many degrees he had, he would always be nothing more than damaged goods.

CHAPTER 26

GOING BACK TO CORONA del Mar I had the sensory illusion that I was returning home. In fact, I was merely returning to a building with four walls, a roof and a door. It did not resemble any kind of home that my parents inhabited or that I grew up in. My wife's and my home was an ostentatious display of wealth where we each inhabited separate parts of the estate.

The illusion was in allowing me to think of it as home. In reality I hadn't had a real home since the onset of my professional life. I didn't believe that out of any sense of self-pity. It was just a fact. I would have had just as much affection for a dung heap, as I did for "our" home.

On the other hand, our home gave my wife the appearance of respectability and social status. For me, it was just a display of what green could buy. Deep inside, I felt no connection to the French provincial furnishings. I thought them effeminate and uncomfortable, if not downright decadent. In spite of my rant, I allowed myself the illusion of feeling at home because it gave me a brief respite of safety, no matter how tortured the illusion was.

I pulled into the garage, entered the kitchen and immediately encountered Consuelo scraping the morning dishes. The bitch always had her wash everything by hand. God forbid if one of her precious Villeroy and Boch dishes was damaged in the dishwasher. I've never understood people who had to eat on fine china. I could have eaten on paper plates and have been happy; I'd even have settled for stoneware.

Consuelo was an enigma. Short and overweight, she could have been the poster girl for a middle aged Hispanic woman who had raised her children and was settling down to enjoy life. Instead, the bitch had her dressed in a black and white starched maid's uniform that emitted a rustling sound as she moved about her duties.

I liked Consuelo. When the bitch was away on one of her many shopping trips to San Francisco, I would take my dinner and eat with Consuelo in the kitchen, on simple glass dishes. I would listen intently to her stories about the little village she came from on the Mexican Peninsula.

It was hard to understand how people could be so poor and have so much self-dignity. She believed in walking across the border and finding a job. She was light years ahead of her fellow villagers. It didn't matter to her what kind of work she did; all work was good no matter how dirty it was. It was troublesome to me that she endured the bitch's personal humiliation, but then I'd never been hungry; never with any sense of desperation.

As I started to walk up to our bedroom, Consuelo hurriedly moved in my direction with a large brown box.

"*Señor* Jake this was left here for you this morning."

Taking the package from her, I could not see any postage marks or FedEx notations. It felt heavy in my hands and I wondered who had sent it. There was no return address. I felt a sense of anxiety. I kept imagining it could be a terrorist bomb or something that would explode. I decided to open it in the privacy of our bedroom.

I felt my hands tremble, as I started to open the box. Then I said to myself, what the fuck? I just tore it open. When I saw what was inside, I was alarmed at the contents. I picked up the accompanying note and found myself reading it over and over again.

"Jake,

I am sending you two Glock 19s and a few other things for your protection. The Austrians make great pistols. This is the smallest version of the Glock and it's easy to conceal on your person. There are six, seventeen shot magazines. If you need something beyond the first magazine you are probably a dead man, but I thought I would give you a little insurance. It's my black sense of humour.

By the way, the ball point pens are not for writing. Sealed inside of each pen is a load of Semtex that encases tiny shards of titanium. The shrapnel is lethal. There is an electronic trigger that is set off when you click the pen. The Semtex is sealed in a plastic housing and has no detection taggant added to it to produce a vapour.

You can probably pass through all but the most sophisticated airport screenings. I would stay away from the large international terminals but, if you do have to use them, come in from a small feeder airport so you don't have to pass through their security.

I am checking with all of my contacts to see who is after you. If you need to talk to me call 843-010-0001. This number does not exist in any government data base. The number will self-destruct after you have used it. Burn this note and crumple the ashes, and then flush them down the toilet. Be careful!

A."

I had forgotten what a sense of empowerment a gun could provide. Conversely, the other side, whoever they were, also had guns. It did not make me feel good to be packing. Even more disturbing were the explosive pens. I wondered who sat up at night creating such devices. A person had to be really screwed up to want to unleash one of these mini bombs. Answering myself, I thought it better to eliminate one of them before they eliminated me.

I sat in our room for a long time. I don't know why I continued to call it "our" room. I never slept there. It was just for display so she could show it off to company.

There always seemed to be an endless stream of people passing through the house. For me they were nondescript; I couldn't tell one from the other. It was kind of like what the Chinese were purported to say: "All round eyes look alike." It was the same way with our friends. In the winter, the women seemed to relish wearing the latest St. John knits, contrasted with Ann Taylor prints in the summer. I never figured out for whom they dressed or even if they were trying to please anyone.

In the back of my mind, I merely thought of them as a bunch of middle aged cows trying to recapture their youth. Their chit-chat was an endless line of prattle about the latest make up that would hide the crow hops around their eyes and spider veins in their legs.

Sometimes I would overhear them babbling about the newest plastic surgeon in town, in their anxious frenzy to get to his gate and obtain the latest body lift.

I don't know why I allowed this crap to continue in my own house except for the fact that divorce was expensive, and I would only be left with half of what I had earned. It was cheaper to just keep her on a leash and let her run. I felt so damn alone.

My life was about bad choices and was about to get worse. I suddenly realized that I had been just sitting in the red leather Natuzzi chair for hours. The room was dark and still. It projected an eerie calm, as if no one lived there and had been empty of inhabitants for a long time.

My attention turned to the bedroom window when I saw a flash that illuminated the night. It was just the streetlight coming on. It startled me because I had been deep in thought. I really did not know what to do or what was taking place in my life. For someone who made his living giving advice to others on how to run their life, business and sweethearts this was a depressing event.

I knew I had to go someplace where it was safe and just think things through, but there was no place I could think of to go.

Walking down the stairs, I entered my study and opened the wall safe. I had forgotten what was in it, save for my passport. I heard the click of the tumblers, cranked the safe handle and opened the door. I found ten grand in cash. I grabbed my passport, the money and threw a bag of casual clothes together.

A taxi took me to John Wayne Airport where I caught a shuttle to LAX. While I was in the shuttle I picked up an L.A. Times someone had left on the seat and found a disturbing article in the national section. Its headline read, **AUTHORITIES FEAR PROMINENT ORANGE COUNTY ATTORNEY MURDERED.** I went on to read the article to see who'd been offed. As I read the Times, my hair began to stand on end. It seemed that the victim's face was crushed beyond recognition, but he had been identified as Jake Mandel from the name sewn into the lining of his suit jacket. I did not like what I was reading.

When I got to LAX there must have been a thousand people milling about in the Bradley Terminal. Most of them were Asians, but there were a few white people. One thing for certain, I did not want to go to Korea or Japan. I would standout like a sore thumb. I tried to think of where I could go where everyone looked like me and I could just merge into the crowd.

CHAPTER 27

MOST AMERICANS THOUGHT ISRAEL was unsafe. They envisioned terrorists around every corner, and bombs under every rock. In truth it was the safest place in the world, save for the occasional terrorist who slipped through the security barrier.

I needed a safe place of refuge while I figured out what to do. Israel was ideal. I thought about taking a Glock and a few of the pens with me but was concerned about passing through Israeli security, lest I be caught with dangerous weapons and treated as a terrorist.

In the back of my mind I could hear Argus cautioning me against the trip, but I was more fearful of doing nothing to improve my security condition.

Being someone's prey was an uneasy feeling, especially when it wasn't clear who the hunter was. I had to protect myself against the unseen.

I walked over to the El Al counter at the Bradley Terminal where there was a huge crowd of people waiting to board the flight. For security purposes, the El Al Jumbo was parked at the far end of the tarmac.

Looking around I spotted four Israeli security guards. They had the appearance of rugged ex-marines who did not quite fit into their civilian clothes. Each was scanning a different part of the boarding party and passengers in the terminal. Locking eyes with one of them, who was about thirty feet away; I gave him a stare and then broke into a smile. He knew that I knew and, from his body language, I felt the exchange of a kindred spirit. I was beginning to feel a little more secure.

Approaching the ticket counter, I brushed up against a very good looking ramp agent. She could not have been more than twenty-two. She seemed to exude heat. I explained to her that I wanted to purchase a last minute ticket, that the trip to Israel was being made on a whim and that I had no luggage beside my little bag with a change of underwear. I could see the bells ringing in her head.

Her friendly demeanour turned to suspicion. Examining my passport, she inquired of my father and grandfather's first names and whether I had any family in Israel.

The next thing I knew, I was led aside to a small interrogation room where she and two guys, who looked like they either came straight out of central casting or from Special Forces, proceeded to interrogate me as to why I wanted to travel to Israel, at the last minute, without any luggage. I had aroused all of their suspicions and they were taking me for someone who was intent on doing bad things. I knew I had to play it straight or I would be sitting in a lockup or worse. They were not to be toyed with.

Taking out my wallet, I displayed my State Bar Card and explained that my wife had been having an affair and that she had decided to leave me for her personal trainer. The affair part with the personal trainer was true, but she would never leave me. It was easier to continue to suck on my tit and enjoy the perks of the good life. She wasn't about to throw that away.

The story was simple and I could tell it with a straight face. My service time in Bosnia was good practice for what followed; a pat down and body search. They were efficient, well trained and impersonal.

Finally I was asked about the ten grand. My explanation was plausible. I said, "I found it in the house safe and I didn't want the bitch to get it."

Everyone had a good laugh. I paid thirty-four hundred dollars for a round trip ticket in coach and was the last one to board the flight.

CHAPTER 28

THE FLIGHT TO TEL Aviv was a *'balagan,'* which doesn't literally translate well from Hebrew to English. The best way is to describe it is "organized chaos in coach." It ranged from the ecumenical Christians gathering in groups of eight near the latrine and carrying on with their prayer session on their way to the holy land, to observant Jews trying to find the correct compass direction to direct their prayers. Kids were running freely in the cabin doing as kids do, with all the shouting and screaming that was attendant to their age.

I did my best to ignore the *balagan* and tried to sleep. Through it all, the flight attendants maintained a gracious attitude and managed to serve three meals. What really struck me was that I saw Christian and Jewish families and they appeared to be having fun, just from the occasion of being together and making their pilgrimage. They did not ask for anyone to entertain them. They amused themselves with their good company and appeared to know their place in life.

It was so fucking different from anything in my life, it caused me to ask myself, what did they know that I didn't, that made them content within? There was no one to answer my question, but at least I thought I was asking the right question.

Once I'd cleared Israeli immigration, I could feel some of the tension come off my back. I knew theirs was the best filter in the world. That did not mean that whoever was hunting me could not get through. It would just be tougher.

I made my way over to the phone store in Ben Gurion Airport and rented a telephone. It gave me two hundred minutes access to the States and unlimited access in Israel. I was beginning to feel better.

Suddenly, I realized it was Friday, darkness was approaching, and everything would be shutting down for the Jewish Sabbath or Shabbat, as the Israeli's call it. I hailed a hack and told the driver I wanted to go to the Aviv Spring Hotel on the Tel Aviv waterfront. He wanted seventy-five bucks to get me there. I hesitated. It was the lawyer in me. I wanted to negotiate.

He left in a flash, saying, "It's Shabbat, I need to get home."

Standing there, I didn't see any other cabs. I felt fucked as I had shot myself in the foot over my damn ego. As I turned to walk back into the terminal and rent a car, I saw a white Mercedes streaking my way. I jumped out of the roadway to avoid being hit. Then the driver stopped, got out of his car, and started cursing at me. I kept talking back to him in a calm voice. His anger vented when he realized I was just one more crazy American.

"I want to go to the Aviv Spring Hotel in Tel Aviv," I said.

"Aviv Spring? There is no Aviv Spring. There is the Aviv Spring Divinci, but it's not the Aviv Spring."

In my broken Hebrew, I asked him, *"Kama Kesef?"*

He responded, "Seventy-five American dollars, but I have to be home, its Shabbat."

I handed him a hundred dollar bill and said, "Please."

It was the same old Aviv Spring. Just the name had been changed. I remembered it as the watering hole for international reporters and had spent many good hours at the bar.

Looking around, I noticed that the bar was gone. In its place was an expanded lobby with uncomfortable chairs. The once proud Aviv Spring could not compete with the many five star hotels on the beach. It had lost its lustre. I suspected that was viewed as progress.

Israeli hotels provided a unique breakfast. The Aviv Spring was no exception. I marvelled at the vast array of fruits, cheeses, breads and eggs. That was part of the Israeli breakfast. Managing to make a pig out of myself, I returned to my room. I had carefully chosen a room on the fifth floor that gave me a clear view of hallway. There was also a fire escape exit right next to the room, so if I had to get out quickly there would be no impediment.

So many pieces of the puzzle were still missing. I didn't even know what the puzzle looked like. Two days had passed with no human interaction. I decided what the fuck? I was going to call Argus. My hands trembled as I dialled the number. Hearing his voice answer the phone was reassuring.

"Jake you're in a lot of danger."

"Where are you now?"

I quickly explained.

"There are too many people in Tel Aviv. You need to go north and spend some time in the Golan Heights. Less people, easier to control, strangers stand out like a sore thumb."

"You're wrong, Argus. I feel secure here."

"Jake, listen to me, you're in deep shit up to your ears. I'm sending you a present. Take a trip to see the ancient village of Katzrin. I can't do any more."

I heard the urgency in his voice and knew that something had gone very wrong. Sometimes, when you didn't know what to do, it was best to do nothing. I sat in my one hundred square foot room and wondered what there was for me to do. I was confused and angry. My life was never much fun, but now it was turning into one fucked up piece of shit.

Looking out the window on the Med, I could see the sun was about to set. It was rapidly getting dark. In four or five hours the pubs and restaurants would be going full swing, but I knew that I was not to partake that evening.

Then there was a hard knocking at my door. I heard, "Room Service. I have a personal delivery for Mr. Mandel."

My gut began to convulse. Was this really Room Service or had my hunter found me? I wasn't in bad shape for a middle age man but I knew no matter how strong I was, a bullet would knock me down.

Cautiously opening the door, I observed one of the Russian maids holding what appeared to be a heavy package. I had seen her working in the hotel in the morning. By evening hours the cleaning staff was usually gone and I wondered who she really was and who had sent her.

I took the package and started to give her a twenty shekel note. She pulled back her hands and laughed.

In broken English, with a heavy Russian accent, she said, "I'm taken care of Mr. Mandel."

I instantly got her meaning. Taking another look at her, I wondered if she had been made up to look like a custodial staff member.

Closing the door, I ripped open the box. My attention was drawn to a simple, unsigned note that read, *"Listen to what I said and do as I said."*

Along with the note I found another Glock and three magazines of ammunition. I was amazed at the depth of Argus' reach.

CHAPTER 29

AVIS WAS A BLOCK away from the hotel. I walked over there early in the morning and picked out a gunmetal grey, Volvo S80. It had the biggest motor on the lot and appeared to be a hardy car. I didn't care about rental expense or fuel economy. I wanted a car that would move when I goosed it.

I told the rental agent I needed to get the car and go before the heat of the day set in. He was disinterested and kept telling me he could not do anything until his computer came online. He appeared as if he had been out all night on the town, and the last thing he wanted to do was show up for work. No matter what I did, I couldn't push him. He ran on his own clock and all I could do was wait.

I took the car for a week, not knowing how long I was going to be in Israel I just had an unexplained feeling that I had to get to the ancient village at Katzrin. It was at least five hours away.

Driving north, I kept looking in my mirror to see if anyone was following me; nothing. I began to feel as if I had overreacted. Then I thought about what Argus said and I found myself looking in the rear view mirror over and over again.

I marvelled at the new development that had taken place. The infrastructure was new and shiny. Looking through the windows of the passing cars, I had a sense their occupants were going about their daily lives with some purpose, other than just eating and shitting another day. Maybe I was projecting my own wants on to them.

The Volvo climbed at a steady pace into the Heights. I stopped to wizz and had a cup of coffee at the Sea of Galilee. The tranquil view of the sea was deceptive. I could see into Lebanon. A thought slipped across my mind. I wondered what the Iranian proxy Hezbollah was plotting now. Regardless of what Iran's proxies did, there was nothing I could do at a personal level to confront their actions. Strange though that I thought about it. In the back of my mind, I also thought about what Rodney King had said, something to the effect of, "Can't we all get along?"

I'd wondered about that myself.

After misreading a few road signs, I finally got to Katzrin. It was five o'clock in the afternoon. The back of my shirt was soaked with sweat; I hadn't taken a spare. The day was quickly cooling down.

I saw a few cars at the entrance to the ancient village. As I parked the Volvo, I slipped the Glock into the back of my waistband and donned a light windbreaker. I didn't know what to expect. For the first time a sense of fear began to pervade my person.

I hadn't been to Katzrin before and I walked into the village not knowing what to expect. The area had been conquered by Israel in the 1967 Six Day War. Until then, it had been forgotten.

The Arabs were late comers to this area, although that did not stop them from claiming it as their own. I listened to a short description of the site on some headsets.

Between 1971 and 1984, the site was excavated. The archaeologists found an ancient synagogue dating back to 400 A.D. The Katzrin Synagogue was built in the 6th century on top of the old synagogue. In 749 A.D. the Golan earthquake occurred and the village was abandoned. The Arabs didn't come along until the 14th century.

I walked into the excavated synagogue. Its southern wall faced Jerusalem and there were two massive stone steps that led to a raised stone platform. Its wooden roof had long ago rotted. As I took in the full panorama of the sanctuary, my eyes focused on the lone figure sitting on a stone bench near one of the walls. I thought for a moment I was experiencing a hallucination and then I realized it was her. It was Aurilane who, in one moment had fallen into my life and, in the next, had disappeared as if she'd never existed.

Her eyes met mine and in the last light of the day we remained transfixed, staring at each other. I didn't know what to do. This was all beyond me.

"We've been watching you for a long time. I've been waiting for you."

I heard her tones and felt myself propelled forward. Pulling her into me I could feel her body begin to convulse. What was I to say? I was a lawyer without words. I held on to her, fearing that at any moment I would awaken and it would all have been an illusion. I felt her heart pounding in her chest and knew that our convergence was more than mere animal lust. With that, all of my social veneering was gone. The lawyer was gone, the need to dominate the situation was gone and the little boy who was really me emerged and began to cry. It was not a cry of pain, but of joy. I was now transparent with another human being, for the first time in my life.

The Poets wrote that the sweetest kiss was when you were sixteen and experienced physical contact for the first time. They got it wrong. I ran my tongue over the roof of her mouth. I knew she was experiencing great sensate pleasure in anticipation of the intermittent contact of my tongue, as well as the climax that was to come.

For the first time in my life, I was not concerned with my own sensual pleasure. My only purpose was to give pleasure to her. This was a new thing for me; an insight I'd never had before. I'd never cared about money or what anything cost, as long as I was pleasured. I'd accumulated wealth without purpose or function. The act of giving without reservation was alien to me, but now I could not give enough.

The Glock in my waistband fell to the ground. She began to laugh.

"Argus was always a bit over dramatic," she said.

"He has a flair for high drama. We would never let anything happen to you here."

With that, she picked up the Glock and placed it in her handbag. I could not believe it, I wasn't making my own decisions. I was being handled; someone else was doing the thinking and I thoroughly loved it. I'd never let anyone take control of my life. Without a moment's hesitation, I had abdicated all personal responsibility.

CHAPTER 30

I FOUND MYSELF FOLLOWING her. She quickly walked to a black Mercedes parked nearby and motioned for me to get in.

"What about my car? I can't just leave it here."

"Leave it. Get in, no one will bother with it."

I felt a moment of hesitation, but the anticipation of being with her again was overwhelming. I found myself simply following her directions and got into her car. A sense of jubilation pervaded my mind.

In an instant, I realized that all the time up to now had been without any real purpose and that perhaps there was hope in my life. My successful career, the accumulation of wealth, my luxurious lifestyle simply faded to grey, in the realization that none of those things made me feel alive. It was only her presence and the promise of tomorrow that gave me a sense of life.

Neither of us spoke as the car tracked the road. I suppose we were each transfixed in our own reality, uncertain of what the next moment would bring.

There was longing in my soul to find absolution as if everything had always been illusory. I'd flitted from one shallow relationship to another, each of which suffered failure. Compensation came in the form of accumulating material things that become the toys of everyday life. The only difference I'd experienced between childhood and adulthood was the price of my toys. I had an epiphany that this was what my life had become. I didn't like it; worse, I felt cheated.

As we drove along, all sort of thoughts raced through my mind. A stranger might have looked at me and felt envy. After all, I had high professional status, vast financial resources and open access to the power brokers in the community. My life was simply a ride on the merry-go-round, with a brass ring at the end of each ride.

The reality had nothing to do with appearance. In point of fact, I was no different than a whore who sold her flesh. In my case, I sold my mind for money. In the case of the whore, she'd let someone use her body for sexual gratification. The critical thinking I performed got strangers out of trouble by letting them walk barefoot through my mind. I could not discern any difference between myself and a street walker. It didn't make me a very happy person. Beneath my steeled exterior, I longed for a mental intimacy that would give me a sense of satisfaction.

It seemed like we drove forever. The reality was that we were only in the car for twenty minutes.

When I felt the Benz slowing, it occurred to me that I had not asked where we were going. We pulled into a small town of quiet streets, illuminated by tall street stanchions that had the appearance of beckoning beacons.

The streets were clean and echoed an appearance of orderliness that could be found in small town America. Before we stopped, I observed a few women with prams walking their children. I later learned that Katzrin was a town of twelve thousand people, mainly populated by military families.

She pulled in front of a house and announced, "We're here."

Looking around I could see a porch light that lit up the front yard of the villa. I followed her to the unlocked front door. We went in and as she fumbled with the light switch I found myself in a living room bathed in a soft white light. She motioned for me to sit down.

As I walked to the corner of the red leather sectional, I could hear my heels as they came in contact with the white marble floor. It made an eerie sound that seemed to fill the entire room.

"I'll just be a minute, I need to freshen up. Make yourself comfortable. If you want a drink, there's a full bar."

With that, she was gone and I found myself alone in the room. Never being timid, I took the measure of the bar and fixed myself a Jack Daniels on the rocks. There was a certain taste to good whiskey that provided a pleasing sense of euphoria. I was not disappointed.

Looking around the room, my eyes focused on its contents. I saw only two pictures. Walking up to the larger coloured print, I saw that it appeared to be an original Calder; I was impressed. I felt I could simply walk into the gauche and escape to another universe. It was hard to take my eyes off of it. I wondered how she'd come into possession of such an original valuable art work.

The other picture was of a young man in a green army uniform, with three bars on his shoulder. I wondered if this was her brother. I could see nothing else of a personal nature. My inspection completed, I sat and waited. That's usually the way it is; men always wait for women. It was part of the chase.

I must have dozed off, because I didn't hear when she came back in. Opening my eyes, I saw her looking at me in an odd kind of way, as if she had not made up her mind as to what our relationship was going to be.

Getting up from my chair, I grabbed her and pulled her to me. I wasn't rough; I just had an eagerness to merge. At that moment, life could not have been better.

The morning came swiftly. There were still so many questions, but it felt like we had forever. I had no eagerness to interrogate her. I just wanted to be with her.

"Jake, I want to show you the town. It'll be fun and we can talk. And you can be like any other silly American tourist."

"Whatever you want, I'm okay with."

I was tired from the night and my body cried out for food. We drove over to a small gas station that doubled as an outdoor café. It was owned by one of the local Druze.

"He makes the best food in all of Israel."

Looking at the outdoor eating tables, it didn't appear to me to be a five star restaurant. I saw a group of seven soldiers seated at an adjacent table. There were two Army tenders parked nearby and the heavily armed soldiers were laughing and eating. Whatever they were eating, it smelled great. They spoke the jingo of Army Hebrew and I could only make out a few words. The military had a way of bastardizing the language.

I let her order. Soon our table was covered with skewers of lamb, French fries, salad, humus and pita. I ate as if I'd never seen food before. I couldn't shovel it into my mouth fast enough. Then I suddenly realized that she was laughing at me.

"I'm glad to see you have a good appetite."

We both started laughing. I guessed that was part of the discovery that couples engage in.

"So, where's my tour? I want to see the sights."

As we drove around to the south, I could see the Sea of Galilee; to the north, Mount Harmon; and to the west, the hills of Upper Galilee. It gave me a feeling of being in Disneyland. This indeed was a sanctuary.

She parked the car and we looked out at the vast expanse that was the Sea of Galilee.

"Jake, I know you want to ask me a lot of questions. You've made me feel a magic that's been gone for years and I want to explain matters to you. At the same time, I can't tell you too much because it's not good for you to know."

I nodded my head as if I understood, but recognized that I understood nothing.

Slowly she said, "I was born in England and went to school there. My father was an investment banker and if, I hadn't met David, I would have led the privileged life of my mother."

I didn't know who David was, but felt like the pieces were falling into place.

"David was a committed Zionist," she continued.

"He believed that his purpose was to move here and make his career in the Army. His father was five years old in 1939 and had been taken to London from Germany on the eve of the Second World War. His grandparents did not escape the *Shoa*. His father's first wife was barren and a second union later in life produced David. I was a blank silly girl with an empty mind. I felt inspired by his sense of purpose."

Paranoia was biting at my soul. I was beginning to wonder if she was married to David and then thought she could not be jumping with me if she was. This kind of woman had too much depth and commitment to engage in casual sexual romps with strangers. Then I thought David must be the army officer in the living room photo. My mood began to change to despair. I knew I had to hear her out. As she spoke, I listened to the sadness in her voice.

"We came here to the Golan because David wanted to live on the frontier. He used to joke that God didn't give Tel Aviv to the Jews. If you want to be a good Jew, you have to live on the frontier."

I heard my lips mumble the words, "Is David the guy I saw in the photo in the living room?" I really did not want to know, but could feel this threat to my happiness.

Looking directly at me, she said, "Yes."

I began to feel that everything was lost. My house of cards was collapsing. In twenty-four hours I had built a fantasy world in my mind and I could feel it crumbling under the weight of her words.

"Jake, please understand that David is gone."

She said it so matter-of-factly I could not discern the meaning of her words. I looked to her for some reassurance.

As if anticipating my question she went on.

"David was killed by a sniper. He was on a routine patrol. They never caught the shooter. I was left here alone and wanted to hit back, but how? That was why I joined the Mossad. With my English education and British passport, I've been very useful."

I was almost afraid to ask, but knew I had to, "Why did you pick up on me when we were on the plane? What do you want from me?"

Choosing her words carefully, she said, "I can't tell you too much or anything that would put you in more danger. We have a lot of trouble with the Iranians. They're the biggest exporter of terrorism. Your friend, Thad Flowers, was a man of many dimensions. There was a defector. Before he was discovered and eliminated, he sent a jump disc to Flowers as an insurance policy to guarantee his safety. The jump disc was sought after by many parties. Flowers' death was not intended by any side. Everyone just wanted the jump disc."

She paused for a moment as if to gather her thoughts. Then she said, "Flowers' associates and his behaviour were watched for a long time. When the jump disc couldn't be found, it was generally assumed that he had somehow transferred it to you, as his best friend. We believe your office was targeted because the other side thought that was the easiest way to destroy the evidence." With that she was silent.

"And us, is there any us?"

A pained expression came over her face.

"Jake, you are a dear sweet man and as you so well understand, I am a woman and I have needs too. But the truth is that even though David is dead, in my heart he will always be the love of my life. I can never change that."

My mind had gone numb. As if from a far distance, I heard myself say, "Is your name even Aurilane?" I didn't know why, but for some reason the answer to that was important to me.

She smiled, although there was a look of sadness on her face. "It's my name for you to know," she said. "That's as real as I can make it."

I also smiled, although it was just a reflexive action. I no longer saw her. She was merely an illusion; a ghost that had passed through me, touched my heart and ripped it out.

Aurilane wondered to herself, *Can there ever be another love in my life? Would such a love mean disloyalty to David? What would David have me do? Does anyone ever get a second chance?*

In a barely audible voice, Jake heard himself say, "And us; is there any us?"

A pained expression came over her face.

"Jake even though David is dead, in my heart he will always be the love of my life. I can never change that. But what I can tell you is that my heart is not so small that I cannot love another. So the question is then, how big is your heart? Must you possess totally, or can you accept that the woman you love, who loves you, can also have love for a man who is no longer of this life? If you can do that, then there just may be an, us."

I seemed unable to hear anything she said, as the ground under my feet gave way. My world spun out of control.

CHAPTER 31

IMAM PARVAIZ WAS HAPPY to be back in Tehran. His exit from the United States was one step ahead of Homeland Security's computer. If he had waited another twenty-four hours, he would have been caught in its net. As it was, he was now safe. Picking up the telephone, he arranged to meet Colonel Mahmoud Nejad Alizadel in the coffee shop across from IRGC headquarters. It was an inconspicuous place and no one would consider anything unusual for an IRGC officer to meet with his spiritual advisor.

"Parvaiz," Mahmoud Alizadel said, "I'm worried about what the Ovasi boy knows. Can he hurt us?"

Parvaiz reflected for a moment before speaking. "He is blind to our operation. He knows nothing about our purpose or why he was given his mission. There is nothing he can say that will uncover us. If he speaks, all he can say is that he carried out a mission for the good of Iran. It doesn't matter what the Americans say about it. We'll just turn it around and call it a lie."

"I'm comforted by your words Parvaiz. You know there are losses in every operation and, no matter what, our operation is still invisible. The Americans may suspect we are up to something, but the boy is a dead end. He served our purpose."

Both men broke into broad smiles and exchanged remembrances of their childhood over a second cup of Turkish coffee.

CHAPTER 32

THE CONSPIRACY HAD BEEN uncovered but the plotters not identified; also, as far as I knew, the jump disk had not been found. Through Argus, I learned that it was considered by all interested parties to have been lost. The search for it had ended and there was no longer any interest in me.

I wouldn't have discussed it with anyone, but I wondered if the package that was marked "Personal and Confidential," I'd received when I'd returned from Houston, might have contained the jump disk. I'd never opened the package and thought perhaps it had been destroyed as a result of the bomb that had been placed in our office building.

Even though our floor had escaped major damage, the effects of the overhead fire sprinklers and the tremendous chaos on the day of the bombing and those days that followed meant that the package was probably tossed out when the office was shut down and later cleaned out before we'd moved to the new location. I'd never know and I didn't want to know. It was over and, as much as I could, I tried to put it all behind me.

* * * * *

BY NOW I HAD RETURNED to the States. While I wasn't overjoyed with the investigation the Feds had done, I nonetheless felt a sigh of relief that it was over.

Now the criminal process would take its course and the facts would be revealed. That was really a joke because so much of the trial process was not designed to reveal the truth, but simply to gain an objective. The newspapers were abuzz with the story. It was inconceivable to me that any defendant could obtain a fair trial in Orange County, let alone these defendants. The result of any trial would be a foregone conclusion.

The conspirators would each have their day in court, but in the end the Federal hammer would come down on them. Their ideological beliefs would not be considered as relevant evidence and their grievances would not be aired in court, save for a statement at sentencing.

As a result of the destruction of the National Bank Building, our firm was officing in a new high rise, trying to put together the broken pieces and lost files of old clients. One of the associates joked that it was like burning down the forest so new trees could get their start. Her words were not kindly received and her next job was with the Probate Division of the County Counsel's Office. I hoped she was able to discern the intent of the dead people she was pondering. Leslie was back to her old self and was still running my life, such as it was.

✳ ✳ ✳ ✳ ✳

THERE WAS A CERTAIN comfort in hearing my intercom buzz. Leslie's voice came across the line. "There's a Dr. Ovasi to see you," she announced.

I didn't remember any appointment with a Dr. Ovasi and looked at my calendar to be certain.

"Never heard of him."

"What does he want?"

"He says it's confidential and he must see you. He seems to be very emotional and appears to be under a lot of pressure. I think you should talk to him and see what he wants. Who knows, it may be interesting to you."

I learned a long time ago not to try and thwart Leslie. She seemed determined that I was going to see this guy no matter what, so I said to myself, *What the hell, I'll give him an audience for 30 minutes.*

"Okay," I said. "Give me a few minutes and then show him in."

Five minutes later Leslie led him through the door.

"Dr. Ovasi, I'm Jake Mandel. What can I do for you?"

As he was starting to speak, I looked him over to take in the full measure of the man. There was a noticeable tremor in his left hand and I could see a nervous twitch in his right eye. He appeared to have trouble framing his words. Finally, in a slow and deliberate manner, he said, "Wally Ovasi is my son. I need your help."

I thought I had seen everything in my years of practice but this kind of dumbfounded me. Wally Ovasi was one of the alleged terrorists who had been arrested for the bombing of the National Bank Building. The inside line, rumoured that the U.S. Attorney had more than enough hard evidence to nail Wally's ass to the wall, as well as the collective asses of his co-terrorists. With all that had happened and considering all I had personally been through, I couldn't believe Wally Ovasi's father was sitting across from me, requesting that I help him.

"Why are you coming to me? I've been deeply involved with this whole mess from the outset. I don't think that I could do your son any good from a professional standpoint."

"Mr. Mandel, you are the only one who can help us, because you were involved. You understand that even the innocent have to run from these people and sometimes they cannot get away. I know that Wally did some terrible things, but he is our only child. My wife is falling apart and I feel like a freight train just ran over me. Our world is upside down. Even if he goes to prison for a long time, at least he won't be dead to us. Do you understand?"

I wasn't sure how to respond.

Finally I said, "Would you like a drink, Dr. Ovasi? I was just about to have a Tanqueray on the rocks. Maybe you would like one too?"

"No, I don't usually drink. Well, maybe just one."

I found myself pouring two doubles with extra ice and handed one to Dr. Ovasi.

"Doctor what you're asking me to do is to put aside all that happened to me personally, to my firm, and to my best friend in the world, and defend your son in a capital murder case. That's a really tall order. But even if I were inclined to do it, I don't think I can get past my own prejudice and be of help to him."

Dr. Ovasi wiped his eyes with his handkerchief, blew his nose and started spasmodically coughing. He appeared like a man who was completely overwhelmed. I felt sorry for him because all he'd wanted was for his son to have a good life.

I didn't believe the doctor had an evil bone in his body. It wasn't his fault that the kid turned out to be a worthless piece of shit, yet I wasn't sure I could tell him that.

I knew what my answer should be, but there was always the temptation that this case might be the great trial that I'd always wanted. Only a trial attorney would have been able to understand that feeling. It was a bloodlust to try the last big case, regardless of the fee. It was like pulling a case through a knothole. Very few attorneys ever got the opportunity and, if the opportunity presented itself, only a fool could have ignored it. I suppose that was why some considered trial attorneys to be no better than whores. If they got the green, they were ready to go. If the case was difficult enough and their ego could overflow and abound, they were ready to go. It was just a matter of being stroked. On the other hand, there were some things for which there was no price, no matter what the case may have portended.

"You have to understand....I'm probably going to be called by the government as a witness to testify in this case. I will be testifying against your son. It would be unethical for me to testify as a witness and place my credibility at issue and, at the same time, try to defend your son. There's an inherent conflict of interest that simply cannot be overcome."

My words fell on deaf ears. I could tell that the doc was not listening to what I said. Like any loving parent, he just wanted to save his son from the needle.

There was nothing I could do to help him. The same was true for any lawyer in our firm. We were simply conflicted and, if we did not voluntarily recuse ourselves, the trial court judge would do it in an ugly way. I didn't need that kind of stress in my life. I merely wanted the return of normalcy and to listen to the printers churning out their endless supply of paper. If that made me jaded, so be it. That was what I wanted.

In as a polite a manner as possible, I heard myself saying, "Doctor, I am really sorry, but there is nothing I can do for you."

As I rose from my chair, I saw the tears streaming down his face. I really wished I could help, but sometimes there is no remedy. I walked him out of my office and proceeded to have another Tanqueray on the rocks.

＊ ＊ ＊ ＊ ＊

I MET GRADY FOR breakfast at Shelly's Tavern. It was a shit hole, but all the trial lawyers without homes would show up there in the morning to sober up over a Bloody Mary and eggs Benedict. I realized I was the same as the rest of the crowd. We all had homes, but were essentially homeless. It was all about making a bad choice in a partner and then repeating it over again with a new partner. When you picked a woman for her looks and nothing else, you got a shallow hull that had the warmth of a piece of modern art. So it went for most of the trial lawyers.

Grady was looking good. Married life seemed to agree with him. He was the only one in our firm that had a successful relationship with a woman. He either had magic or we were just a bunch of schmucks. I didn't really know what it was, but he always appeared to have a stable relationship that allowed him to see things in context.

"Jake this better be about something important! I could be playing with Becky this time of the morning. I think I'd enjoy that a lot more than looking at your ugly puss."

That was Grady, sex on the mind 24/7.

"Look," I said, "I've got a problem I want to discuss with you. I know it's not my problem, but I really feel sorry for this guy. His kid is a piece of shit that should be locked up for the rest of his life, but the parents are innocent and are being crushed."

I briefly related what had transpired. From the look on Grady's face I could swear he must have had my office bugged, because he seemed to know more details than I gave him. I've never understood how information got around the office, but my meeting with Dr. Ovasi was apparently an issue of public discussion.

Grady stared directly into my face.

"We can't touch this case. If we were to get involved, it would destroy our firm and all the people that depend on us to make their living. Besides that, the Rules of Professional Conduct are clear. You cannot be a witness and advocate at the same time. It's first year black letter law. End of issue!"

I knew he was right but I didn't like the answer. I wanted him to give me some magic bullet that would make everything okay. It was like asking God to talk to you when you were alive and the billboard says, "You will meet God when you die!" Perhaps I was getting soft. I hated to think that below my hard exterior there lurked a heart of gold. Well, maybe not gold; I'd have settled for copper.

As a former prosecutor, I also hated the new generation that inhabited my old position. Looking at their blond hair and cherry coloured faces, I experienced difficulty communicating with them. They seemed to come from a privileged class that could spare two years of their lives to do public service in the prosecutor's office. The salary meant nothing to them. They seemed to possess a self-righteous zeal as to right and wrong that was born out of some messianic religious movement. Their currency was prison time and they had no apparent concern with the vagaries of making a living. Somehow that never seemed quite right to me.

The average kid going to law school came out with two hundred thousand dollars in government backed student loans. Then he had to bust his ass eighty hours a week in a civil litigation firm to pay back uncle sugar. He knew what it meant to drive a ten year old car that had a hundred and fifty thousand miles on the motor, and worn tires that looked like racing slicks. Sure he'd have liked to be a prosecutor, but there was no way in hell he'd be able to afford to do it.

Every time I walked into the U.S. Attorney's Office to talk about a case, I'd always get the same old speech. "The government is seeking the maximum. Your client is a no good prick, and you know that Federal Judges don't have discretion to make downward departures from the sentencing guidelines. Why don't you just plead and apply?"

I was always disgusted by that attitude and the prissiness that went with it. For someone who had never been the object of a Federal prosecution, it was impossible for them to understand the awesome power of the government. Even on a high-grade misdemeanour, when the Feds came to make an arrest six U.S. Marshals banged on your door. The exercise of power by the U.S. Attorney mirrored the conduct of the Marshal's Service. The government had a big club and they tended to use it to beat up the little people. It wasn't that I was against enforcing the law. However, I didn't like to see people bullied, no matter what their crime. If the judicial system was going to stand for something, there had to be a level playing field.

I considered what Grady said. It wasn't that I didn't think the kid was a piece of whale shit. It was just that I saw the world from his perspective.

"Grady we really have to do something."

"Jake, you're wrong. A defence lawyer's only obligation is to see to it that his client has a fair trial. He's not there to have his client found factually innocent. The lawyer didn't commit the crime, all he can do is put on the evidence and what happens after that, happens. That's it!"

I guess it was the maverick in me but, in spite of everything that had occurred, I still didn't like the message. I kept thinking about Dr. Ovasi and how his life was destroyed. The American dream had turned into a nightmare for him.

Maybe I was getting soft. I really did not think about the lives the kid had cut short. The system had ceased to make sense to me. Reduced to its elemental forms, the criminal justice system did not work. It was never intended to address political crimes or provide restitution for all of the diverse victims swept up into the criminal enterprise. In its most basic text, it was simply a means of maintaining an order of sorts. It did not address any underlying social issues. I'd often wondered how to invent a better system of crime and punishment but I had no answers.

✳ ✳ ✳ ✳ ✳

THAT EVENING I MET with Grady again. We went in his car, a black Infiniti. The goddamned car was bigger than my Benz. I liked it—the Japanese were giving the Krauts a run for their money.

We drove and talked and found ourselves over at the Waverunner Bar in Newport. It was a kind of a long narrow joint, with a bar that was over a hundred and twenty five years old.

The bartender claimed the bar was brought to California around the Cape of Good Hope and reassembled here. I didn't know if that was true, but a lot of things have gone down over this bar. We were still talking about Dr. Ovasi. I guess I was mumbling to myself and had half of Grady's ear.

We plunked down next to Rick James. He was a retired career prosecutor, still living out of the public trough. I just kept talking and watched Rick eat his dinner.

He told the bar tender, "Jimmy, bring me some tomatoes, lettuce and olive oil." Rick then proceeded to put a little olive oil on the "salad" and pronounced it fit to eat. He commented, "This will coat my stomach so I can drink my dinner."

The young turks had kicked him out of the office. To avoid boredom, he was taking indigent defence cases. He didn't need the money, but he did need the mental activity.

Retirement sucked if a person didn't have outside interests. The problem was that if you were a good trial lawyer, you didn't have the time to develop outside interests. Then, suddenly, you were old and no one wanted you around.

"So what brings you and Grady out tonight?

I would have thought Grady would be banging his squeeze this time of night."

One thing about Rick, he was never particularly discreet in what he said. I could see, as of yet, he had not begun his nightly toot.

"Rick I want to ask you something strictly in a consultation capacity. Is that agreeable to you?"

"Mandel, knock off the shit and speak your mind!"

I rapidly told him as much as I could about Dr. Ovasi. Grady sat mute and just listened.

When I was finished, Rick asked, "Is that all?"

"That's it, except for some minor details." I was a good historian and could have gone on for hours, but I put just enough bait on the hook to get his interest. I could see the wheels going around in his head.

This was a case he couldn't win, but he could really fuck with the government and make the U.S. Attorney look like an idiot. The facts appealed to his dark sense of humour. Besides, it would keep him busy and he would be in the courtroom. This was his stage and he was the thespian.

At one thirty in the morning, Jimmy announced, "Bottoms up."

That was his signal that we should have our last drink and get the hell out of there by two. I told him to give me the bottle and worry about the rest of the patrons. It helped that I put a hundred dollar bill on the bar. At two, he cut the lights and said he wanted to go home. I handed him another hundred and told him, "We'll just be a few more minutes."

The three of us staggered out of the back door of the Waverunner at three in the morning. Good thing the cops were no longer patrolling the bars. They usually caught their last customer at two thirty and then tried to get some shuteye.

I reached into my wallet and gave Rick Dr. Ovasi's card.

"This meeting never happened."

"I don't have any memory of it."

"What you do from now on is on your own, got it?"

"Okay, Jake and thanks."

I watched him as he got into his vintage Jag. I thought for a minute the motor was not going to turn over. Finally, it caught and billowed out a large plume of black smoke that was visible against the xenon light of the back parking lot. With that, he rumbled off into the night.

CHAPTER 33

MY INTERCOM WAS BUZZING, but I still had trouble using the new equipment. There were too many fucking buttons to press. I couldn't figure out how it was set up. When I finally got it to work, I heard Leslie's voice on the line. "Dr. Ovasi to speak with you. He says he's very grateful!"

With that she clicked off and I found myself staring at the phone. The last thing in the world I wanted was any further contact with Dr. Ovasi. You never knew if the Assistant U.S. Attorney was bugging his line. I stared at the phone for a minute, deciding whether or not to take the call. Bravado got the best of me.

"Jake Mandel here."

"Mr. Mandel, this is Dr. Ovasi. I just wanted to tell you how grateful I am to you for helping us."

I knew I had to cut him off and pretended I didn't hear what he had said.

"Dr. Ovasi, I'm late for court. I'm sure if you call back at another time, I'll be able to talk to you."

With that I hung up and stormed into Leslie's space. My look said it all, I didn't even have to open my mouth. The message was clear; under no circumstances was Leslie or anyone else in our office to put any calls through from Dr. Ovasi. I couldn't repair the damage that may have been done, but I absolutely refused to be a victim of my own kind heartedness in helping Ovasi's son.

$*\ *\ *\ *\ *$

LIVING IN ORANGE COUNTY required the adoption of a mentality, as much as it did living in a physical location. Everyone subscribed to the local rag that served as a newspaper. I'd come to doubt that much attention was paid to the first page of national news. There was a preoccupation with local drivel and the society page of the paper.

Running true to form, the paper put out a teaser indicating it would be publishing an exposé of the Ovasi family in its Sunday edition. It promised a first hand account from one of its undercover reporters. The paper claimed it would bring to light the truth involving the Ovasi kid and his family, along with never before seen pictures. I experienced a double reaction. At a reader, I was mentally titillated by the promised exposé. As a lawyer, I was horrified.

No matter how horrific the crime, a defendant was entitled to a fair trial without prejudicial pre-trial publicity. Even the most heinous offender was to be granted that right. The playing field had to be level. Although I was not fond of the U.S. Attorney's Office mentality, I found it hard to conceive they would engage in this kind of conduct, knowing full well that any conviction obtained would be hopelessly compromised by such action. I wondered who was leaking and what their motive was.

$*\ *\ *\ *\ *$

I WAS OVER AT the Federal Courthouse objecting to the certification of a class action lawsuit against one of our Chinese manufacturers. The plaintiffs' attorneys were alleging injury to a countless number of children who they claimed were exposed to chemical toxins from a product our client produced. The Judge wasn't buying into the claim.

Exiting the courtroom, I ran into Rick James. He had a young lawyer in tow, carrying his briefcase and books. She was tall, with high cheekbones, arched eyebrows and pitch black hair that came down to her shoulders. She was wearing a tight black skirt, slit up the side. Of even more interest, she didn't have a wedding band. I wondered who was taking care of her, since I knew Rick had long ago ceased to have any interest in sex.

"Rick aren't you going to introduce me to you friend?"

"Hey, Jake. How you doing?"

Reaching out with my hand and hoping to make contact with her, I exclaimed, "I'm okay."

She did not pick up on the tender.

"Melissa, this is Jake Mandel. He's one of the best, but be careful. He's always trying to get into every girl's pants."

"What can I say?" I shrugged my shoulders and smiled.

She glared, rather than smiled back at me. I mused to myself; *What the hell; you can't hit a home run everyday.*

"Rick, what's gong on today?" I asked.

"Just the usual conflict with the local press. They want to try the Ovasi kid in the papers and bundle him off to death row. Not much different from the yellow journalism of the early 20th century. Bastards never learn!"

I nodded my head in agreement. "I didn't know you were on the Ovasi case."

Rick caught my cue, and responded, "Yes. I was contacted by Dr. Ovasi and he requested me to represent his son. At the time, I didn't think the case was going to be so complex or I would have charged him more. Oh well, I'm on the record and stuck with it so I'll just do the best I can."

The truth of the matter that Rick had just won the first major skirmish in the case, but had a long way to go. The client himself was usually the main obstacle in these types of cases. As it was, this case had political implications and no prosecutor was going to make an offer to plead guilty to a reduced charge.

It took the government about six months to get ready for trial. I think Rick could have tried the case on Day One. The government's resources were unlimited. In contrast, the Ovasi family was quickly exhausting their lifetime savings in the defence of their son.

I heard through the grapevine that Rick had retained a forensic psychiatrist to examine the Ovasi kid and was considering a not guilty by reason of insanity plea.

An NGI case was really tough to defend. In effect, the client admitted to the whole prosecution case. Then he claimed he didn't know what he was doing by reason of a murky mental aberration and should not be accountable for his acts.

Evelyn Schmidt was the head of the local psych society. She had an uncanny knack of not protecting her clients' secrets. If you wanted to hear the latest rumour, coffee with her would give you an earful. Our firm had handled some personal tax issues on her behalf, for which she was immeasurably grateful. She passed on the news about the Ovasi kid. My reaction was to think the case was becoming a train wreck. It was leaking all over the map and I could not imagine how the Wally Ovasi was going to get a fair trial.

CHAPTER 34

THE FEDERAL LOCKUP WAS nothing like Wally had imagined it would be. He found himself in a cage, five feet wide and seven feet long. The ceiling was a mere two inches above his head. A hard bed with an iron frame was anchored to the wall. The toilet was riveted to the floor with an opening that was just large enough to shit in, but not large enough to stick his head in, should he try commit suicide by drowning. There was no window. A single bright light was embedded in the ceiling and remained on twenty-four hours a day.

He was separated from the rest of the facility by a two inch thick stainless steel door that had a narrow slot through which he was fed his daily meals. Recessed in the wall was a fisheye camera and a sensitive microphone connected to a central security room. Wally was watched twenty-four hours a day. A single two inch air vent in the ceiling kept his cell at a constant seventy-two degrees. He had no pillow and no sheet. The white walls of his cell gave no hint of the material beneath the paint. He had the compelling urge to masturbate and relieve the tension in his body, but refused to give his captors the satisfaction of further observation of his private life.

His keepers had taken away all of his personal effects. In place of his clothing, he wore a white, loose fitting gym suit with no string or elastic. He had difficulty in keeping his pants up. No matter, there was no one to dress for.

His watch was gone too and he had no concept of time or how long he had been there. He began to count days, based on the number of breakfasts he had been served. Breakfast consisted of a thin gruel of oatmeal, lunch was a peanut butter sandwich and dinner was a bologna sandwich on stale white bread.

At first he would not eat the food that was tendered to him. Then when he became hungry enough, anything looked good. He would imagine himself in his parents' home, with his mother doting over him and asking what he wanted for dinner. It all seemed so long ago. The reality was that he had only been in custody for ten days.

$$* \; * \; * \; * \; *$$

INSIDE THE DEPARTMENT OF Justice, a heated discussion was taking place between the policy makers and its lawyers. Tamara Mayfield was the assistant head of the DOJ. The exercise of power and the prestige of her position more than compensated for the modest amount of her government salary.

She liked her job because she was insulated from the day to day friction that occurred when DOJ lawyers rubbed up against each other. Today was different. A hot potato had landed on her watch and she was stuck between the CIA, who cared nothing about the civil rights of American citizens, and her own lawyers who were barking at her heels to comply with Federal law. In a fit of self-pity, she thought, I have loftier plans than to simply end my career in this job.

She knew full-well that, unless she got a handle on matters, they would spin out of control and she would be the sacrificial lamb offered as penance for the sins of the administration. The higher-ups would say they knew nothing about what was going on; that she was merely a rogue abomination and not reflective of the culture of the Department of Justice.

The problem was that the CIA had the ear of the President and, together, they would do whatever it took to ensure national security. If rules were bent or not observed, there would eventually be a *"mea culpa"* by a press spokesman for the administration. He would claim that the administration's actions were for the good of the American people and that in times of great national urgency, the rights of the individual had to give way to the greater national purpose. Conversely, there were those civil libertarians in the DOJ who maintained that any compromise with the civil rights of an individual placed the department on a slippery slope from which there was no recovery. That was the question which plagued Tamara; what should she do?

There was no one she could go to for advice. She had not been prepared to make the kind of decision that was necessary and proper in this case. She finally reached the conclusion that whatever she did would be wrong by someone's standards. The real issue was to make a decision that presented the least possible harm to her personally.

It was eleven-forty at night. Picking up the phone, she reached the chief trial deputy at his home. Her message was crisp and pointed.

"This is Tamara Mayfield."

"Yes, ma'am, I recognize your voice. This must be very important or you wouldn't be calling me this late at home."

"Listen to me very carefully!"

"I want Wally Ovasi brought before a U.S. Magistrate first thing in the morning. If you're asked how long he's been in custody, explain that you don't have any information on that, but you can get it. Tell the Magistrate that Ovasi was just turned over to us by another agency and leave it at that. Do you understand?"

"Yes, but what if the Magistrate presses the point? I mean, he might not stand for the explanation I'm giving."

"I don't believe you do understand."

Her words were measured and direct. "I've given you instructions and I expect you to carry them out."

With that, she clicked the line and the call was ended. She slept peacefully. The problem was on someone else's plate and they would have to explain.

CHAPTER 35

IN THE MORNING WALLY was led into the courtroom. There were two heavy chains around his waist and his hands were shackled by handcuffs, locked to his waist chains. His legs were encased in steel clamps that forced him to hobble instead of walk.

He had several weeks of stiff, black beard growth. Instead of appearing like a typical American teenager, he manifested the appearance of a Taliban fighter from the dusty streets of Afghanistan. The appearance he desired had been unintentionally achieved.

The courtroom was punctuated with heavy security. Seven men in blue blazers stood at ramrod attention in the courtroom. Their eyes scanned every window and door, as if sniffing for any hint of trouble. Three uniformed officers stood behind and to the side of Wally. A stranger, seeing this display for the first time would have been dismayed by the arrogant display of power.

The Magistrate read the litany of charges to Wally.

"Do you understand the charges against you, Mr. Ovasi?"

Wally was bewildered by what was taking place. When he entered the room he was already on shaky mental ground. The experience of his arraignment was too much for him. In a barely audible voice he said, "I want to talk to my father."

With that, he slumped down and remained silent.

* * * * *

IT WAS EARLY MORNING. Dew covered parts of the ground around Rick James' California cottage. He didn't like getting up early in the morning, especially when he had really tied one the night before.

Observing himself in the mirror, he had difficult reconciling the person reflected, with his self-concept. The mirror showed a somewhat bent individual with a gaunt appearance, who looked older than Rick's actual age. The years of high profile trials accompanied by heavy drinking, poor diet and chain smoking had taken their toll. His exterior appearance was that of an old man, physically broken by the ravages of time.

In his mind he still thought of himself as a young man on the cusp of a brilliant professional career, out to put the bad guys in jail. He had a mission and purpose.

The reality was that he had been given his death sentence by the oncologist his family practice doctor had referred him to. When he first heard it, he exhibited an aura of denial and disbelief at the medical findings. At the time, he chose to ignore the advice of the oncologist by referring to him as Doctor Quack.

In the back of his mind he knew the clock was ticking down. He could take the advice of the oncologist and the painful chemo-therapy that came with it, or he could have five or six good months and simply fade to grey.

Recalling the conversation with Doctor Quack, an amused smile came to his lips.

"Tell me Doctor, how many of your patients actually survive chemo?"

"That's an unfair question. Survival can mean many things. The life span can be increased; there are all sorts of possibilities."

"Perhaps I asked the wrong question. I want to know how many people you've cured with your chemicals."

Rick thought to himself, *I've got the fucker now; he's not going to be able to wiggle out of this question.*

It seemed an eternity for the doctor to answer. Finally he said, "Okay, Mr. James, you've got me. I can't honestly tell you that anyone was cured. The truth is that all of my patients eventually die. I can prolong life in some instances but, in your case, the quality of life will be less than acceptable."

There was a deafening silence in the room. Rick was a superb advocate and knew how to ask a question to illicit the truth. The problem was that he didn't like the answer. It was as if someone had cut the ground out from under him. He felt himself cascading into a whirlpool from which there was no escape. For the first time in his life, he could not control outcomes. He had no desire to drink the poison cocktail of Dr. Quack, but there were no reasonable alternatives. He found himself engaged in a battle whose outcome was predetermined.

Rick was grateful for the last chance that Jake had given him. It would be his last trial, and he would give it everything he had. In the moment, he was lost in the exhilaration of mentally watching himself perform before the jury. This would be his last and greatest performance.

* * * * *

ENTERING THE FEDERAL LOCKUP, Rick mused at the stench coming from the facility. It didn't seem to bother the inmates or the guards, but then they were used to the odour that comes from confining human beings in small animal cages. The ability to withstand the odour as well as living and working in the lockup environment was a testament to the adaptability of men. Prison life was not the romantic tale of 18th century novelists. It was something he would never get used to.

He approached the jailer in the attorney-bond room and handed him his driver's license and State Bar Card. The jailer hesitated for a moment when he examined the driver's license. The photo in the license bore little resemblance to Rick. The cancer that was ravaging his body was stripping him of what was left of his good looks and appearance.

"It'll be just a moment, Mr. James."

Cutting off the PA, the jailer summoned his Sergeant. In a few minutes a friendly face appeared.

"Rick, how the hell are you? You look great."

Rick felt relieved, and thought, I must still have it, whatever it is. He failed to appreciate what had just occurred.

This morning, he was early enough to see Wally before the count began. Once the count started, all of the inmates would be locked down and he could be waiting for two hours or more for Ovasi. He congratulated himself on his good fortune.

CHAPTER 36

IT WAS RUMOURED THAT George Sandoval was an affirmative action appointment to the Federal Bench. The great grandson of Mexican immigrants, there was nothing Hispanic about him except for his name. In private, his father still referred to him as "Jorge" but never when non-family members were around. His light complexion, blue eyes and sandy brown hair betrayed no hint of his origin. Long ago, his family had intermarried with the Anglo population.

* * * * *

IT HAD BEEN AN election year and the democratic President had hopes for capturing a large segment of the recent Hispanic immigrants who had begun to populate Orange County. The President had needed a token to demonstrate to the newly minted citizens that he was with them. Orange County was very important and the votes from down south could be enough to swing the balance, enabling him to carry California in the November election.

No one got to be President without some street smarts, as politics was the business of appearances and promises. It didn't really matter what the outcome of any particular event would be, so long as appearances were maintained and promises were made to ensure re-election. After the election, the outcome of any issue or event could be spun to blame the other side for the failure of the promised outcome; if only the other side would have acted in a responsible manner and did their public duty. There seemed to be no real difference between the Democrats and Republicans; they were merely two faces of the same coin.

Summoning his Appointments Secretary, the President explained his dilemma.

"Spencer we've got to carry Orange County in order to win California. I've been giving it a lot of thought and we need every Mexican we can get to vote."

Spencer had been the loyal dog of the President for many years. Still, he found it unnerving to hear the President refer to Hispanics as, 'Mexicans.' It did not fit the public persona of the President and he feared that one day the President would slip up, which would be disastrous.

"Well, Mr. President we have an open Federal Judgeship that's just been funded."

"Maybe we can find a local Hispanic lawyer who's active in the Orange County community to fill the spot."

"It just might work."

"Spencer, I knew I could count on you. Take care of it!"

Five telephone calls and twenty-four hours later, an exasperated Spencer met with the President.

"Mr. President we've run into a stone wall. I called my sources and the only thing we can come up with is a guy by the name of George Sandoval. He's kind of a playboy and not a very serious lawyer. The only thing Hispanic about him is his last name."

"Spencer I can't believe what you're telling me. Is that the best you can do?"

"I'm sorry, Mr. President, but it is."

"Well, I suppose we can teach him to be a 'Mexican.'"

Spencer recoiled at what he was hearing, but in the bawdy world of politics recognized where his bread was buttered.

George Sandoval was quietly summoned to Washington, and put on a private jet. No one would ever know he had been there or why. Not only did he leave Washington with new ties to Hispanic life, but his mentors succeeded in prepping him for his Senate Confirmation Hearing. As it had always been, the fixers had done their job.

✳ ✳ ✳ ✳ ✳

SEVEN YEARS LATER, FEDERAL Judge George Sandoval was assigned to hear the case of the United States v. Wally Ovasi.

CHAPTER 37

THINKING BACK TO HIS childhood, Rick could not remember a time when he was not in fear.

The psyches said the earliest conditioning was the imprint that stayed with a person all their life and it didn't matter what they did to try and escape from it. In the deep recesses of his mind, the fear was real and always there, and it was always with Rick.

Over the years, he had learned to mask his apprehension. It helped that he was a revered member of the establishment, because those less informed would never doubt his station and resolve. Those in his adopted class were not eager to peer too closely, lest their own inadequacies and insecurities be revealed.

Rick lovingly recalled his father. He was a gentle man who spent his life in the service of the Methodist ministry. There was a time when Rick did not look kindly upon the image of his father. When he was young he thought his father weak and ineffectual. In his maturity, he recognized that to stand up for what is right often made the individual appear weak and ineffectual when compared to the awesome power wielded by politicos.

The truth of the matter was that the power of the state was ineffectual when opposed to the act of personal resistance to wrongful authority. It took Rick a lifetime to recognize this truth.

The Second World War changed many lives. Most alterations were not for the better. Rick's parents lived in a small rural town in western San Bernardino County, in southern California. As a child, he felt imprisoned by a set of invisible walls that separated him from the rest of urban America. He longed for the big city and the social justice he believed would accompany his move.

At his core, Rick's father was a pacifist. He did not believe the exercise of violence was justifiable under any conditions. Luckily, he was too young to be called to arms in the First World War. By the time of Hitler's conquests, he had found his calling as a Methodist Minister. Given his strongly held personal views, it really would not have mattered what church he affiliated with. For him, the church was more than a mere pulpit. It represented an opportunity to take the moral high ground and stand for something he called "good."

As the war news darkened, the roundup of Japanese-Americans commenced. Rick's father was horrified that the government would take such actions against its own citizens. He found it difficult to intellectually distinguish his government's action from that taken by the Germans, although he was quick to point out that the Germans' brutality and crimes were unmeasured. Nonetheless, it deeply troubled him to see what was happening.

In protest, he led a parade of ten through the main street of the town. Each person carried a homemade sign denouncing the government for what it had done to its Japanese-Americans citizens. The response of the townspeople was to call him a Nazi sympathizer, and to threaten the well-being of his family.

His father's sermons preached that every man had free will to make ethical choices as to how he would live his life, and that God did not assert his omnipotent power over individuals to control life choices. Ultimately, it was the individual who was accountable for his actions.

The response of the wartime government was the surreptitious investigation by faceless bureaucrats from an anonymous government agency, followed by a not so friendly knock on the family door.

As a boy, there was one particular night that Rick could not wash out of his mind. It was late in the evening. From the deep sleep of innocent childhood he heard a pounding on the door. Crawling out of his sleep, he slowly made his way to the railing of the second floor.

That allowed him an unobstructed view of the foyer and front door. His father was at the door. In the pale light of the forty-five watt porch bulb he could make out four men. They were wearing Sunday suits and their heads were covered with wide brimmed hats pulled low over their foreheads. Rick could smell the lingering odour of their Mennen Skin Bracer, as its pungent fragrance wafted into his parents' home. In an instant, he knew they were G Men. Fear began to creep through him. He knew from listening to the radio that G Men only hunted bank robbers, criminals and spies. He couldn't imagine what they were they doing at his house.

The stillness of the night was punctuated by the staccato voice of one of the G Men. Rick could not make out who was talking, but the words were unmistakable.

"We've been watching you. We know all about you. You've been warned."

With that, as if in lockstep, they pivoted and walked away.

The expression on the face of Rick's father said it all. His pale white skin turned a beady red and, as he closed the door, his body movements were accentuated and abrupt.

Rick's childhood and adolescence were coloured by the psychosis of that event. Even as an educated man, he could never wrap his mind around the facts of his history and bring himself to trust the government.

That had been the first of many late evening knocks on the door. What was even more chilling was the constant surveillance of the physical activities of his father. There always seemed to be a 1939 grey Plymouth lurking in the background. It kept a respectful distance, but followed him in his daily activities. Rick remembered seeing one person driving and the other taking what he thought were feverish notes. The grey Plymouth became a constant companion, yet it did not stop his father's protests.

When Rick's father received a note from the Bishop instructing that he cease his protest activities, even that did not deter him. He mused to Rick's mother that the Bishop had simply lost his way.

His protests and the responses of the government began to wear on Rick's father. At forty-nine he suffered a death dealing, massive heart attack.

The war was over, but the government continued its surveillance activities.

Rick's father was now suspected of having been a communist. McCarthyism was on the rise.

Rick's mother was a gentle soul. She could not maintain the crusade of her husband and her only thought was to safeguard the welfare of the children. Moving to San Francisco, she met Mr. James. He was an older gentleman who had never married. Although financially successful, he recognized the hole in his life and eagerly adopted Rick and his siblings. The name of Rick's father was struck from the lineage. Rick assumed a new identity, but, in the back of his mind, he always remembered who he was and where he came from. He swore one day he would even the score.

CHAPTER 38

MRS. OVASI CAST AN elegant appearance, despite her bloodshot eyes and tearful demeanour. Looking at her, Rick could sense she was a woman who was used to getting her way, regardless of the obstacles facing her.

She exhibited the bearing of newly minted wealth that opined everything and anything was for sale and could be acquired, if only the right price was offered. She made a stunning appearance in her white blouse, blue St. John knit and red heels. About her neck was a delicate Yurman necklace, complimented by a flawless large diamond set in platinum which graced her hand. It emphasized her long fingers and French manicured nails. Any stranger seeing her for the first time might wonder who was paying for her.

Aside from her clothing and accessories, she had an air of unreality about her person, causing anyone who engaged her in a conversation to wonder what asylum she had escaped from. Rick was amused by her.

"Mr. James," Chris Ovasi exclaimed, "you are going to get our son off, aren't you?"

Rick could see her husband jerk back in surprise at the tone of her voice.

Dr. Ovasi wasn't concerned about the question itself or that the desired answer that was inherent in it. He had however been made uncomfortable by how it had been asked. He wasn't sure his wife understood the gratitude and thankfulness she should feel towards Mr. James for taking Wally's case.

Rick's eyes travelled back to Mrs. Ovasi, although he did not immediately respond to her question. He continued to stare at her. Her long hair did not fit a woman her age. Likewise, the soft hands and well manicured nails indicated she was a woman who had not done any physical work for many years, yet she seemed to have good muscle tone and her face displayed no signs of aging. Mrs. Ovasi looked to be a consummate consumer who exhibited more than a little self-indulgence. Rick would have to be very careful with regard to any explanation he gave to her.

There was a deafening silence in the room.

Carefully choosing his words, he turned his full attention to her.

"Mrs. Ovasi if you were going to have open heart surgery, I don't think you would demand a detailed explanation from your surgeon as to the precise mechanics of the operation. Think of your son's case as if it were a surgical procedure. Having been around physicians all of your adult life, I'm sure you appreciate that every operation involves a little different encounter, and the surgeon really doesn't know what he's going to find until he opens the patient up. In your son's case, we have a long way to go and a lot of discovery to conduct before we'll know what our final approach will be. But you can be assured that I am going to exercise every Constitutional right he has to be certain he gets a fair trial. If I were to tell you anything else about the defence strategy, that would constitute a waiver of the attorney work product privilege. If that were to occur, the U.S. Attorney could force you to disclose everything you've learned from me and the information you have would not be protected from peering eyes. You would seriously damage your son!"

Rick watched her eyes as he explained what was to come. When he discussed the problem of waiver, he observed the constriction in her eyes and knew he would have no further problems from her. Still, she had raised an interesting question for which he had no real answer. In the recesses of his mind he understood that a conventional defence was doomed to failure. Perhaps he had to play the role of the oncologist who handed out his poison in non-lethal doses, keeping the patient alive but with no guarantee of a cure. He knew the government would spare no resources in order to put the needle in Wally's arm.

The remainder of their meeting grew terse, as Rick explained, "The defence of your boy is going to be very complex. We're going to need a variety of expert witnesses. I've done some preliminary financial estimates. I'll need a hundred thousand dollars within the next forty-eight hours to start retaining experts for our side. Is that something that's manageable?"

Dr. Ovasi took out his Wells Fargo Money Market Account check book.

"To whom should I make the check payable?"

"Make it to Rick James, Client Trust Account. By the way…please understand this is just a down payment for costs. I don't have a full handle yet on what the real costs of experts are going to be, but at least we've got a starting point."

"Whatever you require Mr. James. I want you to understand, the money will be there."

Reaching out to take the check Rick stood up and, as if on cue, the Ovasis also got to their feet and made their exit.

Rick put the check in his safe and took out a small, black leather journal. He began to write.

- Not sure what to do
- Bad case
- Bad facts
- Nowhere to go
- Parents want reassurance of maximalist defence
- Sometimes there is no defence
- Need to come up with something
- No // Will come up with something

With that, he put the book back in the safe until further thoughts emerged.

CHAPTER 39

A LONG LINE OF Supreme Court cases instructed prosecutors that they had to turn over all exculpatory evidence to the defence. In many instances, the prosecutor wanted to hide the good evidence.

In Wally's case, there was no, "good evidence." All of the evidence simply affirmed his guilt.

The brass in the office cackled at the thought of presenting this case to a jury. The presentation didn't require a brain surgeon; any second year law student could have made the case. The U.S. Attorney fully expected Rick to try and continue the case for as long as possible, hoping the delay would work to the advantage of the defence.

* * * * *

I N THE COURTROOM, JUDGE Sandoval maintained a friendly demeanour.

"Good morning counsel. I understand that Mr. James is going to request a trial date some eight months down the road, to give him adequate time to prepare the defence of his client."

"Begging the Court's pardon your Honour, that is not the case. On behalf of Mr. Ovasi, demand is made for a speedy trial in compliance with the Constitutional mandate guaranteeing him that right. I'm thinking about five weeks from today."

The Assistant U.S. Attorney felt like he'd just been hit with a sledge hammer, coming out of nowhere. He jumped to his feet.

"Your Honour, we can't possibly be ready in five weeks. This is a massive case and requires a great deal of preparation. I can't imagine how the defence thinks it can be ready in so short a time. It's simply out of the question."

Judge Sandoval, with somewhat of a benign smile on his face, turned his full attention to the Assistant U.S. Attorney.

"Is the United States willing to entertain reasonable bail for this defendant? As you know, by that I mean bail in an amount he can reach that will put him on the bricks, out of custody."

Rick was amused at the reaction of the Assistant U.S. Attorney.

"Your Honour, it's the position of the United States that this is a no bail remand case. Our position has not changed!"

The slight smile faded from the Judge's lips.

"In that case, trial is set five weeks from today. Please submit any voir dire questions you wish the Court to inquire about with prospective jurors at least five days before trial. The Clerk has my Scheduling Order. Pick up your copy on your way out. By the way, I strongly suggest that each of you read my little blue book of rules and procedures that I expect both sides to observe in this case."

There was no question that the Judge was finished with the Ovasi case for now, as he turned and said, "Madam Clerk, what's the next case on the docket?"

Rick knew he had struck a raw nerve. He could see the bewilderment on the face of opposing counsel and wished he could be privy to the debriefing that was about to take place in the prosecutor's office. He had shaken the walls of the establishment. The prosecution would be forced to re-examine every factual aspect of their case in expedited time.

Rick also had no doubt that his personal movements were being observed and recorded, but for now the hook had been baited.

CHAPTER 40

THE THOUGHT OF RICK'S father was never far from his mind. He had now lived long beyond his father's span of years and his life experiences were much broader than his father's had been. He had seen the best and the worst in people, over a wide range of social classes.

The kernel that remained with him was his father's sense of fairness, coupled with the anger and bitterness of having to grow up without a father who had loved him without reservation. The scar was a roadmap that spanned all the years. He could no more relinquish it, than live with it. It had become a part of his inner self and drove the madness of his remaining time.

Rick had no concern that someone might consider his intended activities the folly of malpractice, nor did he worry about what would happen to his estate. There was nothing anyone could do to stop him.

He held no strong political beliefs, except an abiding contempt for those in power, and those who exercised power in the name of national preservation. He had become a nihilist and, in his own pursuit of excellence, would do all he could to damage the existing social order.

His prior career as a prosecutor could be viewed as a contradiction in terms, or an attempt to go after the really bad people. Now, he was not only the thespian, but the writer and director of the masked ball. No one could foresee what he was about to do.

His plan was simple in its conception and complex in its application. As an incidental matter it would preserve the life of the Ovasi boy for an extended period of time, albeit the quality of his life would be in the toilet. Rick was not an Indian medicine man, nor was he a proctologist. He was a mere legal oncologist who would provide little extensions of life and a delay of the imposition of the sentence. In effect his was a screen play, written to delay the poisoning of his client.

In considering Mrs. Ovasi's comments, a wry smile appeared on his face. Mrs. Ovasi failed to understand his job was not to get her son off, but rather to see to that he received due process. Rick planned to do more than that, but less than what she mandated.

Five weeks out from trial, and Wally had stopped shaving and refused all cosmetic applications for his hair. He began to look more and more like a Taliban fighter in the mountains of Afghanistan. Initially, Rick was not particularly concerned about Wally's appearance, but mentally noted he would have to be cleaned up by the time of trial day. Rick recorded a memo to himself to have Mrs. Ovasi purchase some slacks and jackets for Wally's trial, with the intention of presenting him as the kid around the corner.

Factually, there was no defence to the charges, but that was not how Rick intended to defend the case. He intended to make cutting edge law through the use of a psychological defence that had never before been tendered. He held no honest belief that Judge Sandoval would allow the defence, but he knew the judge could not prevent him from making a record. If the Judge refused to allow him to put on this defence, the high probability was that the 9th Circuit Court of Appeals would reverse, remand and allow the defence to go forward. It wasn't exactly being freed of the charges, but Wally Ovasi's life would go on in spurts and stops and he would live to see several more sunrises. It was unfortunate that Wally had no window.

Staring at his telephone, Rick picked up the handset and rapidly dialed Karl Sussman. Sussman was his friend of many years. Although born of Jewish parents, he considered himself an agnostic and believed there were no absolutes in life. Everything was relative and good and evil did not exist in his lexicon. There was simply life, action, and reaction, without any judgment as to whether the result was good, bad or indifferent. Sussman was the ultimate voyeur. His pleasure in life came from the examination of conduct and its consequential result.

After several rings Rick heard him pickup the line and a tentative voice answered, "Sussman."

"Karl, how the hell are you?"

There was a moment of silence. Finally Karl spoke, "Why are you calling me this late at night? What's so important that it can't wait?"

Rick knew he had to choose his words carefully. He was mindful of the fact that Sussman had completed medical school at Harvard, as well as a PhD in psychology from USC. Of late, he had dabbled in psychoanalysis, having concluded that all he could do as a psychiatrist was to dispense pills and keep patients medicated in a drug induced stupor.

Karl had often expressed the opinion that witch doctors were more cognizant of the inner workings of the mind than modern medical practitioners. Nonetheless, he was highly regarded in the medical community. Not for his outspoken views and criticisms of modern medical practice, but for his brilliance in explaining the inner workings of the mind.

"Karl I'm working on a strange case that I need your help with. You may have read something in the paper about it. It involves the Ovasi kid who acted as an Iranian agent."

Karl did not immediately respond. When he did, his comments were contradictory to everything Rick believed he knew about him.

"Why do you think I should help some kid who's a foreign agent bent on destroying our country?"

Rick was dumbfounded. He wondered if Karl had become a nationalist and how he could have been so mistaken about him and his beliefs.

"Karl this is not about the flag, motherhood and apple pie. This kid may be the Rosetta Stone that's going to make it possible for you to peer into the inner workings of the mind, in a way that's never been explored."

Rick had baited the cage and all that remained was to see if he could get Karl to enter the wire box. In a few more minutes of conversation, Rick could hear Karl feverishly making notes and listened as he thereafter explained to Rick that he would require a team of experts to assist him.

"Don't worry Karl, money is no problem. Ovasi's parents will pop for whatever you need. Just give me the names and CVs of the people on the team and I'll arrange for everything else."

All that remained now was to obtain the co-operation of Wally Ovasi.

* * * * *

THEY SAT TRANSFIXED IN the attorney bond section of the lock up and stared at each other. There was no point in mincing words. As he gazed at Wally, Rick wondered what kind of stupid fuck would go out and commit this kind of crime. No matter; he was the vehicle for Rick's last performance. It would be fun, it would be amusing and in the end, Wally was merely cannon meat for him.

"Wally I can't save you, but I can keep you alive for a long time. I'm also not here to pass judgment on you, because I don't care what you did. Other people though are not as kind in their view. They see you as an evil person who isn't fit to walk the face of the earth. They want to erase you. Your only option is to fight for your life.....if your life means anything to you. And know that each day that you live is one more day than you would have had. I don't have any magic that's going to get you out of this mess, but I believe we can raise a defence that has never before been offered and you might live as much as ten more years before they come for you. That's all I've got. If you want it tell me, but know that I'll expect you to co-operate and do everything I instruct you to do. If not, I'm out of here and you can have the Federal Public Defender. Your choice."

"I'll do whatever you tell me. Just don't let them kill me!"

✳ ✳ ✳ ✳ ✳

KARL SUSSMAN WAS A GENIUS. It was as if he had reinvented the theoretical basis of Psycho-Biology.

He had taken it from a descriptive science to a predictable discipline, where the same results would be obtained if the experiment were repeated.

After hiring his team of experts, they had crawled through every corner of Wally's mind, both physically and chemically. Sussman had concluded with what he believed to be absolute certainty that Wally's behaviour was as a result of his actual genetic structure that no amount of cultural conditioning could have countered. He would testify that while Wally appeared to be normal, he could prove that Wally's genetics and chemistry predisposed him to be a true believer who acted out his belief system by violent means.

To have found him guilty of the crimes he was accused of, and have him executed, would have been the same as killing an animal who hunted, simply because other animals had to die to ensure its survival. If he were an animal and ventured into a human populated area he would be found, darted, and returned to the wild.

Because he was a human being whose genetics and radical belief system mandated his action, to impose the death penalty would be the same as destroying an animal merely because the animal hunted and killed for food. If found guilty, Wally should not be killed by the state for following his genetic imprint, but should be removed from human populated areas and locked up for the rest of his life, as there was no wilderness to which he could be returned.

Rick was very pleased with their progress, even though the vigour of the cancer was taking its toll on him. He wondered if he would really get to finish the trial. The mere thought of it breathed new life into him, increasing his stamina and will to see it through. Chaos would rein.

* * * * *

A WEEK BEFORE THE trial, Rick visited Wally at the lockup. He was shocked by what he saw. In a short period of time Wally's youthful appearance had changed. His face had a puffy roundness that was often associated with a high carbohydrate, fatty diet lacking in protein.

Rick noted that Wally walked into the room, Koran in hand. He ignored that and instead said, "Wally, what's going on with the beard and the white skull cap?"

"*Salam,* Rick. Thank you for coming to see me."

Rick froze. He knew that things were different. Something had occurred that radically altered Wally's demeanour. His whole manner of speech had changed.

"Wally you've got to clean up your act. I've done my part and put the team together that's going to save your sorry ass, but this Muslim shit has to go. I see things I don't like. I can't help you if you're not going to help yourself. Are we on the same page?"

"You just don't understand," Wally said slowly, as if speaking to a child. "When you're in jail you have a lot of time to think. At first, you fantasize what it would be like to be outside the walls that confine you. Then you think about what's really important in life. That's what I've been doing. That's all I have been doing. I realize now that you want me to be something that I'm not."

There was a stony silence. Rick had seen this before in other defendants who'd found God while in jail.

He could build the perfect match box, but if Wally decided not to play, the game was over. There were some clients who were simply not controllable and no matter what was done, they would not act in their own self interest. All he could do was to put the case on and attempt to control as many outcomes as possible.

* * * * *

THE DAY OF THE TRIAL arrived and there was still some doubt in Rick's mind as to what Wally was going to do.

When Rick's time came for opening statement he slowly rose to his feet and addressed the Court.

"Your Honour, the defence reserves its right to make an opening statement after the conclusion of the United States' case."

At least he'd able to preserve Wally's rights until the last minute.

The prosecution began its case in a methodical way that did not miss a beat. Here and there Rick scored a victory by skilful advocacy but, in his heart, he knew that he had not broken the prosecution's case. There was a difference between courtroom flare and destruction of a witness through skilful cross-examination. In his mind, Rick was certain that the Assistant U.S. Attorney would tie the knot, unless there was a sudden change in the demeanour of his client.

Wally sat stoically through the trial, clutching his Koran, his white skull cap pulled low over his forehead.

Without his book he would have made a good appearance for a comical Gillette Razor ad. As it was, he simply appeared as one more sinister Islamic terrorist.

CHAPTER 41

THERE WAS A SEVERE storm on the Newport coast. It was unusual for this time of the year. The wind driven rain pounded everything from side to side. Trees were torn from their roots and the old overhead three-way light at the entrance to Pacific Coast Highway gyrated in a nonsensical movement that fluctuated with the direction of the storm.

It was the kind of day that made me long to have a home with a fireplace and a warm woman to rub up against. I had the home and the fireplace, but lacked the warm woman. Oh, well. What the hell, I thought. I knew I couldn't have it all!

It was getting dark and I decided to stop at the Waverunner. Who knows, maybe I'd be able to pick up some hot bird. Parking as close as I could to the entrance, I got out of my Benz and ran for the door. The parking lot was a mess. Deep puddles of water filled the depressions in the old asphalt paving. For all the money the fucking owners made from the bar, they should have repaved the parking lot. But then, this was capitalism. The formula was simple, use the parking lot in its dangerous condition until someone got hurt, then deny negligence, report the claim to the insurance company and make it someone else's problem. In spite of it being totally corrupt, I loved our system. It made it possible for people like me, not only to survive, but to prosper.

I saw Rick sitting at the horseshoe booth at the back of the bar. His silhouette made a wispy impression in the shadowy light. Looking at him closely, he only resembled the Rick I had known for so many years. The shape of the face was still present, but it appeared gaunt and the skin was tightly drawn across his cheeks and neck. As I approached him, I observed that the fatty tissue which accumulated with age was almost entirely gone. In its place, Rick appeared to exude a mummy-like appearance. The onslaught of death was fast approaching.

I almost felt guilty. In the mail that day I had received a letter from Dr. Death, who had taken the kidney biopsy to test me for multiple myeloma. The results were negative, although he wanted to see me again in six months. I decided that was a good thing, since it didn't require me to do anything immediately. I wasn't sure whether to 'God bless', or goddamn the quack. But I did know, unlike Rick, at that particular moment in time I didn't have to accept my own mortality.

Rick had a drink in hand with a backup on the table. I didn't see any other faces I wanted to sit across from, so I kept walking until I was within his hearing.

"Mind if I sit down and join you?"

"Hey Jake, come sit!"

"You look like you're caring the weight of the world on your shoulders."

For a minute there was only silence. Then Rick looked up and in a matter of fact voice said, "The kid's case is turning to shit."

He didn't have to tell me which case it was; I knew. In the pit of my stomach I felt bad for him. I did not care about the Ovasi kid. This was about Rick. I always believed that eventually every trial lawyer came to the end of the line and wanted to go out on his own terms, because he had already made all of the horrible compromises that life mandated. The last performance was the time to squeeze and grind the other side so that you would not be forgotten in the lifetime of your adversaries. That was all a man could do. Only a few people could be President and life wasn't about riding a white horse at the head of a victorious army. It was about making that final statement and making every word count, as if it were a bullet crashing through the heart of your opponent.

I sensed Rick's pain and knew there was nothing I could do about it. It was all a matter of happenstance. I still wanted to say something that would diminish his suffering, although I knew words were just shallow expressions of intent.

About the same time I sat down, the bartender brought me a glass of my usual poison. It warmed my throat and I signalled to him to bring another. The good thing about always hanging out at the same watering hole was that staff paid attention to your likes and dislikes and tried to please you, all in the name of profit, of course.

I turned my attention to Rick.

"I see you're in a lot of pain, but something you taught me years ago you seem to have forgotten. You did not make the facts or commit the crime. All you can do is put on the case and let the chips fall where they may. I never forgot what you told me and you need to remember it too. Actually, I remembered something else that happened today. You want to hear about it?"

Rick almost smiled.

"Am I going to like this?"

"Goddamn, you are going to love it. I got word today that Trey Stewart piece of shit, walked. And you know why; because Grady is a fucking great attorney. The son of a bitch Sheriff kept Trey in custody for almost eighty hours and moved him from jail to jail. He deprived Trey of his right to an attorney. After Grady talked to the little prick, he tracked the movements and transfers that were done to keep him hidden."

"Wasn't there any court involvement?"

"Damn right there was. The judge was highly pissed because the Sheriff disregarded his order to bring the kid in for a bail hearing, although he could have let that slide, because he usually does. But Grady is not to be fucked with, just as you are not to be fucked with. He took each Deputy Sheriff that Trey came into contact with and nailed his ass to the wall, one ass at a time. While he couldn't get any of them to testify that they knew shit, Grady was able to show that collectively, they didn't know shit for more than three days. The

Judge's highly pissed attitude turned to rage and he threw out the entire confession. That completely shot down the Sheriff's case, because the only reason for hiding Trey out for so long was to get that confession. Otherwise, they didn't have diddly-shit."

"Does it look like they'll re-file?"

"I don't think so. As far as the child's death, it was a he said, she said between Trey and the baby's mother. There was no hard evidence as to who was responsible. It was similar for the drug charges. The Sheriff had nothing except the word of a police informant who wanted to keep his ass out of jail, and would say anything. And you know what, just maybe a baby killer and a drug dealer got off. But Grady can't be worrying about that. He did his job and that's what he was supposed to do. Maybe if the Sheriff had done his job, he would have had a real case. But he wanted to do it the easy way, get good headlines and move on."

"So you don't have any problem with this kid being released?"

"Not one. And I don't think you do either, because the law was followed, although not by the Sheriff. Besides, if anyone has a worry, I'll give you 100 to 1 odds that Trey will screw up again. And I suspect this time the Sheriff just might do his job right. Trey's an arrogant little prick and I have no doubt that eventually he'll find a cell that he can call home, for a very long time. Just like you said, the chips will fall where they may."

Rick smiled and burst into laughter, although it had a kind of hollow sound.

"God, I love the law."

Then he raised his glass in a toast.

"Let the chips fall where they may!"

Although I'd made Rick laugh and I saw some light in his eyes, I still knew life was never pretty and never ended well, and would not do so for him. I kept those thoughts to myself and did not express them to Rick.

"Jake I've never asked anyone for a favour, but there is something I want from you. I want you to come and sit in on Ovasi's case when I put on the defence. I need you to be in the courtroom—to be an affirmation from a real lawyer that I've done my job."

There was a tone of desperation in his voice. I could sense how difficult it was for him to ask. How could I deny him this request?

"I'll be there," I said.

I was to play the assigned role of critic of the play. Relative to his performance, I knew he would hang on my every word as it belched from my mouth. No one should have that kind of power.

∗ ∗ ∗ ∗ ∗

IT WAS TEN-THIRTY in the morning and the prosecution had just concluded its case. Judge Sandoval was not insensitive to the needs of the defence and ordered a recess until two in the afternoon. The jury was sequestered and instructed to return after the recess.

From his raised bench, Judge Sandoval looked down at the participants.

"Mr. James, the Court will expect your opening statement when we resume proceedings this afternoon. Can you give the Court as estimate as to how long you anticipate the defence case to take?"

Rick stood up to address the Court, "I believe we will be here for another two weeks taking direct testimony and at this point, I am uncertain as to what rebuttal testimony will be offered."

"Thank you Mr. James. Court is adjoined until two o'clock.

Rick turned to Wally and said, "We need to talk."

A heated discussion followed and, at its conclusion, Rick was still uncertain of Wally's intentions. When they returned to the courtroom, Rick scanned the notes of his opening statement. Over the break he had changed his shirt and tie, because the one from the morning was sweated through. But, on looking at himself in a mirror, he decided it would be good to change his entire outfit so as to make a cleaner appearance.

The jury had returned and Judge Sandoval said, "All jurors are present as well as the five alternates. Are you ready to precede Mr. James?"

Rick and Wally Ovasi both rose to their feet. Before Rick could address the Court, Wally blurted out, "I am firing Mr. James and have decided to represent myself."

Judge Sandoval appeared to be stunned. He quickly excused the jurors and ordered them to return to the jury room. He wanted to avoid a mistrial at all costs.

"Mr. James, did you know this was going to occur?"

In a barely audible voice, Rick responded, "No, Your Honour."

"Mr. Ovasi, discharging your attorney in a capital murder case is a very serious event. It is not one to be lightly undertaken. You are up against highly skilled and experienced counsel and the results in this case are potentially catastrophic for you. Before the Court will entertain such a request, it's incumbent upon the Court to make a searching inquiry and determine your competence to represent yourself. In that process the Court will also examine your mental capacity to be certain you understand the nature of your actions."

With that said, Judge Sandoval began his inquiry of Wally Ovasi. When the clock struck six-ten p. m. his questions concluded. He ordered all parties to return the following day.

CHAPTER 42

THE FEDERAL COURTHOUSE IN Orange County, as elsewhere, was a living testament to the power and majesty of the United States. In every sense of the word its grandeur was comparable to a Roman Temple of the Gods. At the same time, it had more than national symbolic significance, because it was the ultimate forum to uphold the rights of men and protect each individual from arbitrary state action.

Its staffing was a contradiction in terms because, in order to become a part of the life blood of the Court, the candidate must have appeared to be politically correct, while expressing a professional view in keeping with what was considered to be main-stream or centre of the road.

The reality was that no one could see into another person's mind and determine if their thoughts were evasive. More often than seemed possible, what to outward appearances portended to be the appointment of a conservative jurist, who publicly acclaimed he would not judicially create new law, turned out to be a staunch protector of individual rights. Judge Sandoval was a stark example of that principal. He had risen to the circumstance of his position.

Wally stared at Judge Sandoval. He looked deep into his face for a sign of Sandoval's Hispanic origins. What he saw was inconsistent with Sandoval's name and stated ethnicity. Reflected back at him was a fair skinned, blue eyed man with brown hair and Caucasian features. Wally was appalled by his appearance. It undercut his beliefs to think that this Mexican Judge could undermine the system, while he pretends to be part of the mainstream American establishment.

To himself, Wally whispered, *"Praise be to God that I found the right path to salvation and am not like this judge."* He rocked back and forth in his chair repeating the same thing to himself so as to drown out all of the competing voices in his head.

"Mr. Ovasi, this Court has carefully considered your request to discharge Mr. James as your attorney. Although the Court is not in agreement with you that this is the best course of action to pursue, the Court is going to allow it and you may represent yourself. The Court is going to order that Mr. James remain as an advisor on technical issues, should you require technical legal assistance. With that said, you may make your opening statement or call your first witness."

No one was prepared for what came next. Wally had changed into a traditional Islamic Smock of the religious people. The robe seemed to flow around his body. His head was covered with a knitted white skull cap that contrasted with his brown hair. The moment of decision was at hand. It was the moment Wally's parents dreaded and which those in Revolutionary Guard cheered on, but publicly disavowed.

Wally stood. He knew he had to carefully choose his words.

"I am a soldier of Iran. I do not plead guilty to any crime because it is America that started this war of genocide against the Iranian people. I have killed in the defence of Allah and my beloved country. A soldier cannot be guilty of murder because it is not murder to kill in defence of one's county and religion. I do not disavow my heritage. I am not a hyphenated American. If you want to be an African-American or a Mexican-American or any other kind of American, that is your choice. I am a soldier of Iran! You have the physical power to do with me as you will, but my soul is pure and only Allah can judge me."

A hushed silence fell over the courtroom. It was destroyed by the rush of exiting reporters. They had their lead story for the afternoon news.

* * * * *

RICK DIED TWO DAYS later. The emergency room doctor said his heart gave out but, to those of us who knew him, it was clear that he had just given up and faded away.

Perhaps there was no last hurrah and we just slipped into oblivion, followed by a few kind words from a minister who never personally knew us. Then dirt was shovelled in his face. For those who believed in Heaven, I had a bridge I could sell them.

* * * * *

WALLY'S TRIAL MADE A quick run for the finish line. He was found guilty on all charges and sentencing was set for forty-five days from the conclusion of the trial. Everyone wondered what was going to happen to him. The bookmakers were giving odds of 1,000 to 1 that he was going to get the needle. That was something I decided I wouldn't bank on. Every judge became his own kind of asshole with a direct pipeline to God. I didn't think Sandoval was any different.

* * * * *

AS GOSSIP RAN RAMPANT, I heard on good authority that Mrs. Ovasi was shopping for a family law attorney. It seemed she was ready to dump the doc and try and get a fresh start.

I felt sorry for Mo. He only did what he believed would protect his family in this incredibly screwed up world.

* * * * *

I WAS IN THE packed courtroom when Wally Ovasi's sentence was handed down. I thought Rick would have wanted me to be there. Wally's father sat silently, his hands clenched in his lap as his eyes overflowed with tears; he seemed not to notice anyone except Wally. There was no sign of Mrs. Ovasi.

When all the players had hit their mark, the Judge instructed Wally to stand and then proceeded to hand down his sentences. The litany of punishments followed the list of findings of guilt. It seemed to take forever, although in reality twenty-seven minutes later it was all over. That even provided ample time for Wally's last rant.

Basically, if Wally could have been executed for each soul lost in the bombing of the National Bank Building, he'd have set the record for deaths and resurrections. As it was, he would only get the needle once.

When I thought about it, I decided the outcome would probably have made Rick laugh. Wally still had years of appeals ahead and, while maybe not the ten Rick had wanted to get him, more than enough to move closer to his God.

Wally had left torn, dead and dying in his wake and he would be humanely put to sleep, as if he was a beloved pet suffering from an incurable cancer, which was not far from the truth. Justice once again would be served.

EPILOGUE

MY WIFE WAS LONG gone with more than half of my fortune. Yet, the money was meaningless to me. I realized that there were few things in the world that were as they appeared to be, but Aurilane was not one of them.

She had been totally honest with me and, because I did not know how to handle that, I'd let her go. I understood now. Love was not the same thing as possession. I could not expect her to empty her heart for me alone, as she could not expect me to deny the life I had already lived.

I looked at my watch. Customs was slow. It didn't matter. Soon I would push through the door and enter the main terminal at Ben Gurion Airport. Then my life would begin again as I gathered Aurilane into my arms.

END

ABOUT THE AUTHOR

ROSS GALLEN

Ross Gallen was born in New York and raised in California. Growing up during the turbulent Soviet / US nuclear era, he was acutely aware of the lack of civil liberties in the Soviet hegemony. This ingrained a lifelong belief that the Constitution was all that protected ordinary Americans from arbitrary government action. His writing career began as an Op.Ed. writer for his high school newspaper. Graduating from the University of Redlands, he simultaneously received a Bachelor of Science degree in Geology and a Bachelor of Arts in Sociology. After a short stint in graduate school at the University of California, he proceeded to Cal Western Law School where he earned his Juris Doctor Degree.

Ross is a member of the State Bar of California and the State Bar of Texas. Employed as a Deputy District Attorney he argued the landmark case of *In re Kay* before the California Supreme Court. He honed his skills as a trial lawyer by working as a deputy Public Defender representing clients charged with capital murder and serious felony crimes, and then went on to become a managing partner in a civil litigation firm. He has been a Judge Pro Tem of the Orange County Superior Court and is recognized as a pre-eminent lawyer in the Martindale-Hubbell Bar Register of Pre-eminent Lawyers in America. Ross currently devotes his time to writing fiction and practicing law.